Metaphorosis

September 2018

Beautifully made speculative fiction

Also from Metaphorosis Books

Reading 5X5: Readers' Edition
Reading 5X5: Writers' Edition

Best Vegan Science Fiction & Fantasy

Best Vegan SFF of 2017
Best Vegan SFF of 2016

Metaphorosis Magazine

Metaphorosis: Best of 2017
Metaphorosis: Best of 2016
Metaphorosis 2017: The Complete stories
Metaphorosis 2016: Nearly Complete Stories
Monthly issues

by B. Morris Allen

Susurrus
Allenthology: Volume I
Tocsin: and other stories
Start with Stones: collected stories
Metaphorosis: a collection of stories

Metaphorosis

September 2018

---

edited by
B. Morris Allen

Metaphorosis Books

Neskowin

ISSN: 2573-136X (online)
ISBN: 978-1-64076-116-2 (e-book)
ISBN: 978-1-64076-117-9 (paperback)

September 2018

Graven Image

B. Morris Allen

It's about impressions. First impressions, last impressions, the creased and corrugated impressions that life leaves on our skin as it wears us down to our essentials, and eventually to nothing. I know about impressions; I'm in sales now.

Back then I was a lonely xenoarchaeologist, chasing down one more faded rumour, one more mystery worn flat by repetition and examination. Study, publish, repeat, as postgrads say, until there's nothing left to say, no iota of meaning left unexamined. And there's always something to say.

I'd found mention of the temple in *Henbro's Analects, Volume CLMXIV* (General Era 7,829), and in *Studies of Alien Ruins in the Gortheran Quadrant, #234* (GE 9,237), and again in Borhin's *A Complete Compendium of Religious Structures of a Cubic Nature* (GE 13,943). Eventually, I traced down thousands of other mentions in the literature. None of them had anything interesting to say about it — cursory mentions of indecipherable carvings, a lackluster image of a bare stone cube, and coordinates, should anyone care enough to visit.

Graduate students feed on the crumbs left by larger mouths, hoovering up just enough academic nutrition to keep the system running. By the time they have their degrees, grads have learned to live on nothing, but learned nothing about how to harvest their own food.

I was as desperate as any other postgrad. I'd scrimped and saved throughout college and university, borrowed, cheated, gambled — anything to raise enough money to buy a ship. And I'd done it. A battered, creaking, barely functional S-class scout with no spare parts and a solid-state drive that made ominous clunks despite a lack of moving parts.

I'd saved that simple temple for myself, cobbling together a doctoral thesis from dribs and drabs of nothing, dressed up to look like data. I'd seen, of course, what greater, more tenured minds had not, because that's what postgrads always need to see. I'd seen that the temple looked the same in every image. From crude tri-Ds in GE 3,113 to full-immersion expeers a decade old, the temple stood unchanged. As the sea around it fell, as jungle grew and shrank, as jagged ridges cracked into place above it, the temple never changed. Very slightly rounder, perhaps, the pile of dust at its base a tiny quantum higher, but essentially the same, over 20,000 years.

I wasn't the first to spot the temple's durability, of course. Dozens of others had examined it, analyzed it, determined the stone it was built from was stone, and put the building's longevity down to good engineering and good luck. They interviewed the place's addled but taciturn occupant, learned nothing, and let it go; Methuselan species were a dime a dozen. If one chose to live in the building as a curator of sorts, that was its own business.

They all missed the point, the one crucial datum that would make my reputation, or at least get me a published paper — the dust. In all those images, all those expeers, the dust never moved, never changed, except to grow infinitesimally higher.

The dust was thickest below the carvings; the carvings that millennia of xenoarchs had examined, dismissed, and nonetheless speculated about in reams and reams of dry and ultimately baseless paper. Here there had been change — with every visit, every visual record, the dust grew slightly higher, in peaked drifts that slowly, slowly accreted, clinging to the stone at the base of the temple's single altar like moss determined to reach the top.

In all those centuries, through all the upheavals of flora and climate and land, the dust never moved.

I landed with a screech of sliding metal and a feeling that the landing gear might be, so to speak, on its last legs. I lowered the ship to maintenance level, belly-down in the grass, more confident of a risky zero-base liftoff than of the gear's structural integrity. I had to exit through an alternate port and climb down handholds rubbed slick by age, but safe is safe.

The temple was just as advertised, a nondescript cube of grey stone with a soft fringe of dust at its base. A dark square in the center of one wall marked the single entry to its faded secrets. The curator's yellow tentacles flickered briefly into view as if tasting the scent of ship and woman. Everything just the way every recording showed. No surprises.

The temple was set in the center of a broad sward of teal grass, like a crumb of basalt in a malachite locket. At the far end, the land fell off sharply to a clear pink lake. On the sides, stately growths of brown and beige reached smooth arms up to a light indigo sky. Behind us, a ridge rose sharply up to a plateau. It was beautiful, or would have been if there hadn't been hundreds like it on other, more central worlds.

I gathered my gear from where I'd dumped it out the port, a paltry selection of third-hand analyzers and limited-memory recorders that were all my budget could afford. I strapped, snapped, and inserted until I could find no further excuse for delay.

Closeup, the temple looked the same. The dust beside the door formed the subtly serrated ridges familiar from weeks of study and analysis, from days of repeated viewing en route. I readied an ancient handheld analyzer, but a tremor from the doorway caught my eye, a slow undulation of yellow, like blond hair in a summer breeze. The Curator.

Every report said it was senile, so old and decrepit as to make no sense, kept alive by sheer inertia, too befuddled to leave, too dull to die. Simple manners, however, suggested a greeting might do no harm.

"Greetings, Curator." I said. Not deathless oratory, but it served the purpose.

The thing clacked and hooted and grumbled, slowly waving its tentacles like a hydra, or a Ganulan whispertree. It spoke Common; the records agreed on that. But only when it chose to, and seldom sensibly. It liked visitors, but not imagers, the records suggested.

I shrugged. I'd paid my respects, and I'd yet to turn on my recorders.

Behind the curator's thick stalk, the temple was empty but for the waist-high cube of an altar and its skirt of dust. A thick pane of some transparent stone above provided ample light. I stepped into the entry, and the Curator obligingly flowed aside, its ruffled skin streaming up the near side to form new tentacles as old ones deliquesced into its far surface. It was surprisingly beguiling, like an endless stream of rose petals blown by a gentle breeze. I gave it a smile and a half-bow as I stepped past it.

"Welcome," it said, quite clearly.

I missed my step, turned back in surprise as I struggled for balance.

"Did... Hel... Thank you," I settled on, at last.

"Welcome," it repeated.

"Thank you," I said again, for lack of a better idea. "You're the Curator, are you?"

Yellow tentacles waved, and a rustle of petals rippled round its trunk.

"Okay. What can you tell me about the temple?"

"Welcome." The sound issued from a tangle of yellow limbs, or a ruffle of skin, or some organ deep in the stalk. It seemed to vary.

"The temple hasn't changed," I tried. "For millennia."

Tentacles undulated in an intangible wind.

"Can you explain? How does the temple remain?"

Silence. I tried again, and again, but made no progress. 'Welcome,' then, was the one word it knew, or could remember. Senescence comes to all creatures, even those that live for eons.

"Right, then." I turned away, tried one last time. "What about the dust?" It seemed a topic unlikely to engage the threadbare fibers of a timeworn mind, but it was my topic, after all.

"No image." The thing's smooth tone seemed harsher, more insistent, if no more coherent.

"That's alright. I won't take any recordings just yet, okay? What can you tell me about the dust?" The Curator had my full attention again, and it seemed to me that its yellow skin was rumpled, the waves sweeping faster, like buttercups on a rippling pond.

"Image," it said. "No image." Was there a greenish tinge to the yellow now?

"Can't quite make your mind up, eh?" Cruelty is attractive, when we're the ones being cruel.

We went around for another quarter hour, but I coaxed no more revelations from it, no further expansions of its vocabulary. At last, I turned back to the altar.

It was a waist-high cube of blackish stone, greenish at the edges, but smoother and more rounded than the grey of the exterior. Its surface was smooth as well, with the faintest of sinuous lines suggesting where etching might once have formed gullies and trenches among broad plateaus of stone. Some lines were darker, depressions just barely tangible to a questing hand. I swept my fingers gently across the surface, watching the Curator from the corner of my eye. It stood unchanged, the green shade faded back to golden yellow, the squalls to flurries of bright petals.

There were two places where the relief of the surface was more perceptible. Scratches, even a notch, perhaps. They formed jagged, awkward lines unlike the faintly visible twists and graceful curves of what I assumed to be original carving. Careless equipment mounting, I assumed, or even graffiti; even xenoarchs are people, and some people are fools. The last expedition I'd encountered in the literature had been a decade or more back. The scratches seemed fresher than that, but clearly the temple was made of resistant stuff.

Eventually, the sightseeing complete, I squatted to take my first look at my real subject – the altar's petticoats of dust. The dust formed a fringe of diminutive scree, its gentle slopes looped down here into mild valleys, shaped up there into squat peaks. The tallest stood proud of the others by a centimeter or more, a spike among bumps. It seemed sharper, taller than the images I recalled, and I pulled up the latest record on my left lens. I twitched to an overlay, and yes, the new peak was higher, by a good centimeter or more. Or the altar and virtually everything else had sunk, but that seemed unlikely, and was easily contradicted by a comparison with the other peaks.

My hand trembled as I reached for a sampler. I'd done a meticulous analysis of dust levels in previous records. No peak had grown more than a millimeter per year, and here was a rate ten times that! Not only had I found my footnote in history, but perhaps a moment of glory – a speech at a sector conference, and perhaps more.

A glance at the Curator confirmed that it had not moved, though the undulant petals swayed even more than before. I opened my sample vial, gripped my polished spatula with nervous fingers.

But wait! What was I doing? Sweat slicked my temples as I realized I'd almost compromised my own great find before recording it. I rocked back on my heels, swallowing hard. Almost! Almost, glory had fallen prey to careless ambition, as so often happens when even an expert loses sight of the forest in the glory of the trees.

I took a moment to rest, letting my breathing calm. When my heart had slowed to a rate closer to its norm, I peeled a recorder from its holdstrip and aimed it at the altar dust. "Keep it together," I told myself, and turned it on.

"No image!" The Curator swirled in a squeal of tangled limbs. "No image! No image!" It held its ground, coming no closer, but roils of harsh green swept through its skin, petals suddenly compressed to buds, emerald pustules on citrine muscle.

I turned off the recorder, and watching long tentacles flailing like whips above my head. No prior expedition had mentioned this. They'd described the Curator as feeble and harmless, a fuddled entity of inoffensive mien. This was something different.

I shuffled back from the altar as the Curator calmed, or so it seemed. The thing's petals unfurled again to a carpet of ruffles, their color fading slowly from lime to lemon. I stood carefully, sliding the recorder conspicuously into a pocket.

"No image," I said, holding out bare hands.

"Welcome," it said, in sighs and crackles.

"Not as much as I'd hoped," I said with a hint of smile. No offense; a little joke among friends.

"Welcome," it insisted. A spiral pleat crinkled around its trunk and was gone.

Any good xenoarch studies some biology and physiology. You have to, to interpret relics. I might be a very small fish in the archaeological world, but I was a good one, to use a mixed but biological metaphor. It seemed to me that I might have stumbled on a second good thing here. Other expeditions, including some with biologists, had discounted the Curator. The biologists had instead waxed enthusiastic over the planet's balanced ecosystem, the adaptability of species, the motility of lignolithic graveltrees. Demented singleton sapients were of lesser interest, apparently, even to postgrads.

The Curator, however, was exhibiting a dramatic change in behaviour, a change not noted in twenty millenia of casual reference. Surely that meant something. Yet, while more aggressive and insistent than records noted, it had not said much. If it conveyed its point more forcefully than in the past, it provided little information. A mystery, but perhaps not a great one. Awkward, no doubt, but not an absolute barrier to my investigation. Also a handy backup discovery to keep in my pocket in case of need. Dust, though, was my focus.

Wary, I squatted again, and shuffled my way slowly toward the altar. The Curator stood rooted to the spot, even as I slowly, very slowly, withdrew my sample vial and spatula. No reaction. I had a basic image from the recorder, I rationalized. That would be enough to document my discovery.

I held the vial close to the tall peak of dust, and ever so gently slid the tip of my spatula into the rising edge of one side. The Curator made no sound, and, with almost imperceptible shudders, I transferred my precious grains of dust to the sample vial. My touch was delicate enough, it seemed; the peak held, forming no avalanche to fill the tiny gap in its supporting slope.

I capped the vial and leaned back. Colored swirls formed across my vision, and I realized I'd been holding my breath the whole time I was sampling. I closed my eyes and waited until the colors faded away.

I slipped the vial into a chest pocket, sealed the pocket closed, held it tight with my hand. If the Curator objected, I thought I might escape to the ship with my sample intact. I stood, the altar between me and the mysterious creature. My peak was just below one of the scratches in the altar surface, I realized. From this angle, the scratch seemed cruder, more visible, more evidently purposeful. It started in the faint shadow of an older swirl, jagged sharp left, then down toward the edge, then left again, like the rift from a recent earthquake. It ended just above the peak I had sampled.

Curious, I leant forward. Pulling a thread from my well-used uniform, I tied it to my spatula to form a simple plumb-line. The coincidence of scratch and dust was exact — as exact as could be, with such a crude instrument.

I hovered close over the end of the scratch, aware as ever now of the Curator, but it swayed calmly in its place, seemingly unconcerned.

In the canyon of the scratch were particles of black dust. I fumbled free another vial, set my spatula into the scratch, and traced it from start to finish. A little fall of dust spat out of the crevice and into my vial.

"No image," said the Curator woodenly.

I froze, my eyes straining up to see, but the thing stood calmly, petals unfurled, limbs graceful arcs above it.

"No image," I agreed, definite.

It said nothing, and I straightened in a slow, measured rise.

"No image," I repeated, for good measure. There was no answer, and I skirted the altar, keeping it between us as long as I could. At length, I stood beside the altar, the Curator to my right, the door free before me.

"No image," I said, and bolted.

I was halfway to the ship before I risked a look back. The Curator had flowed back to its position in the doorway, but showed no sign of following. I took no chances, running until I could clamber back up the slippery side of my ship and in through the port. The Curator was unmoved, and I took a moment to watch it. It was an impressive sight, its yellow bright against the grey of the temple, and harmonizing nicely with the teal grass and pink lake beyond. An alien place, but a beautiful one.

I opened a foodpack, and let it steam gently while I labeled my vials and set a grain from each in a battered, century old analyzer. I forced myself not to look at the screen as the machine chugged and whiffled and posted results one by one. Dinner was braised magna beans on a slab of Alerian gelbark, with a beaker of gleanberry juice to wash it down. I let it slide past my tongue untasted, attention fixed firmly on the noisy machine behind me.

Rock, it said, when I turned at last. Specifically, amphibole composed largely of arfvedsonite – a conglomeration of silicon, oxygen, iron, and sodium. Rare on some worlds, common on others. Other expeditions had found no local supply of the stone, and no trace of the builders, which was a minor mystery, but vanished civilizations don't inspire corporate funders as much as picturesque temples, and that was as far as the investigation of origins had gone.

That ground had been trodden further than I could go with my limited means. What mattered to me was that the grains were the same. The dust from the altar skirt was the same as that from the scratch on its top. Not coincidence, then. The one was the source of the other. That was interesting indeed.

Or was it? My heart, which had crept slowly up toward my throat, came sliding back down to my belly. Who was to say there was any meaning to it? Probably the scratches were just what they looked like — graffiti. The planet wasn't exactly on the main routes; in fact, it was in something of a galactic hinterland, but it could be reached. I'd proven that just by coming here.

The Curator must know. It was always here. Presuming it had a memory, of course. Perhaps all it retained were its point and counterpoint of "welcome" and "no image", grooves worn deep into its placid mind.

In any case, I had evidence that dust and altar were of the same material. That was step one in my investigation, and a solid one. I ate my plate (guaranteed nutritious, but it still tasted more of carboard than cake) and went to bed satisfied, if not happy.

I woke the next day with a renewed enthusiasm. My gamble had paid off. A long trip into nowhere, and already I'd gathered important data, with a possible biological footnote to boot. Excellent progress! I could taste the professorship already. Secure in my solitude, I stuck my tongue out and waggled it back and forth. Definitely a professorship. Maybe even associate-flavored.

I ate, washed, dressed, and arranged my gadgets. I'd already decided not to aggravate the Curator more than necessary. I stuck a recorder deep in an inside pocket and threaded an optic fiber out to the front of my coveralls, virtually invisible against a seam. I switched the recorder on, tested the playback. Everything worked fine. I switched off again until I could get outside. No sense wasting limited memory.

The outside was the same. The sky, a slightly lighter shade than before, shaded the grass a little toward turquoise, and I switched the recorder on again just to have a memento. I could always delete extraneous bits later.

As I walked toward the temple, I caught glimpses of the Curator, long tentacles waving languidly at first, then faster and faster until they were almost frantic. The creature pushed out to the door of the temple, leaning out farther than it had done the day before. Like a tongue, I remembered, and flickered mine in response.

"No image," it cried. "No image. No image! NO image!" Its cries grew louder as I approached, its frenzied gestures almost angry now. I stopped, well clear of the door and the Curator's long tentacles. It seemed unwilling to leave the shelter of the temple, and I realized I'd seen no reports of it ever being outside. Someone had remarked on it some millennia back, in fact, and it now seemed accepted that the creature was in some way tied to the building.

"No image," it said again, almost plaintive. "Welcome. No image." Its surface was a striated bilious green now, and the buds had disappeared altogether, leaving a surface slick and solid as muscle. It writhed in place, leaning as far out of the door as it could, its base tight to the temple stone, its tentacles holding it in place, agitated ripples running back and forth in gruesome shivers.

"Alright, alright," I mumbled at last. "No image." I slipped a hand into my pocket, switched off the recorder. "I don't know how you could tell, but no image."

The moment the recorder switched off, the creature calmed. I could see the tension slipping away as tentacles relaxed, the trunk righted itself, and the angry green faded to gold.

"Welcome," it said at last, as the petals re-emerged from its skin. It flowed back a step, welcoming.

I switched the recorder on again.

The reaction was instant. The tentacles flailed, and the Curator's rich skin flushed with the vile green. "No image," it said. "No image, no image, no image!"

I turned the recorder off.

The green faded away. "Welcome," it said, and wagged its tentacles. Like a child beaten by its parents, I thought, recalling customs in the late Althantic period. Bruised, battered, but still hopeful. Still looking for love from its single source of joy and pain.

I turned the recorder on. The Custodian went through its routine, its pleading, colouring frenzy of waving and crying. It made no move to stop me, even standing aside as I walked up, entered, exited again. I could hear it calling as I walked around the outside of the temple, noting drifts of dust, seeing how the teal of the grassy lawn stopped well short of the temple walls, leaving bare the rock supporting it.

When I came back around to the front, I turned the recorder off. I had enough data, and I'd had enough of the pleading. Truth be told, I'd had enough of myself. Grotesque, demented alien it might be, but it had feelings, that was clear enough. And I'd been toying with them for the sake of knowledge.

"I'm sorry," I said, as I watched the creature transform again from green to gold. "I just... I was selfish." I had been, and I could think of no justification. "Humanity at its best."

"Welcome," it said, with a graceful bow of tentacles.

"Yeah." I felt a sudden urge to rip the recorder off, to throw it off, over the cliff and into the pink lake below. But data was data, even when evilly gathered. Ignorance served no one. I contemplated that slippery slope, the Curator rustling at my back, the lake enticing before me, and then I let it go. "What can I say, Squiggly? I'm weak."

"Welcome."

I couldn't face it again, so I went around the outside to the back of the temple. The dust there looked similar, but grey instead of the greenish black of the altar. I scooped out vial and spatula, and squatted down to take a sample from a drift I knew I had captured well in the recorder. Human frailty, or a desire to make the Curator's suffering meaningful?

With a nasty, grating sound, the spatula scooped nothing. Instead of the fine, powder of the altar dust, this was hard. Hard as rock, in fact. I stared at it, befuddled. Perhaps it wasn't dust at all, but a growth, an excrescence, a crust. A secretion, if the temple were a living creature, like mucus dried around its eyelashes. Seepage — that was the word I wanted. Mineral seepage.

And yet, it looked like dust. I'd made a minor study of dust settlement forms on the voyage out. This looked like dust, piled high by droppage from above, and forming peaks depending on the mass, shape, and coefficient of friction of the individual particles. Seepage didn't work that way, but crept up or out, or effloresced in a centered pattern.

I jabbed at the little dust hill, gently at first, then harder and harder, but nothing changed except that the fine tip of my spatula dented. I hadn't even loosen one grain.

Here was my answer, I realized bitterly. The reason the dust never changed. It wasn't dust, but rock, somehow formed to look just like dust. One of nature's little jokes, or perhaps one by the long-gone builders. I threw down my spatula in disgust and went to the cliff to look at the lake.

Almost immediately, I was back. The pattern changed. The piles of dust grew over time. Slowly, but they did. The dust of the altar in particular had … The altar!

I'd had no trouble there. Altar dust behaved like dust.

I grabbed up my spatula, slid it into a pocket. It was useless now for sampling, but I could clean it, and I had others. Vial in hand, I raced back around the temple to the entry.

"Welcome," said my yellow friend.

"Welcome," I answered, and pushed past a stray tentacle toward the altar. Its skin felt warm, like spring sunshine.

I skipped around the altar to the back. The little pile of dust I had sampled had slumped, filling in the spot where I had sampled. The distribution was different, but the peak seemed even higher than before. I sampled again, extracting a tenth of a gram with no difficulty, and slipping it into a vial. The peak shifted again.

I looked up at the scratch in the altar top, to find it fringed with dust again. I sampled some, even as I realized what it meant.

"You're doing this, aren't you?" I asked as I straightened.

The Curator stood silent.

"You're making these scratches!" I looked around. The floor was bare, smooth stone. There! In the corner, behind the Curator, a rusty scrap of metal. I leaped toward it. A piece of wire, discarded by some expedition or other, and now put to other uses. The tip was shiny. I waved it at the Curator triumphantly. "You've been scratching on the altar!"

"Welcome," it said languidly.

This was a find! Far more important than the damned dust. Here I had the dust creator itself! The Curator, the ancient, disregarded denizen of the temple, was responsible for the carvings. At least, for the new ones. Doubt assailed me as I recalled that the new, jagged scratches were quite different from the original, sinuous ones. Nonetheless — Curator, temple, etching. My fortune was made.

"Way to go, curator. Way ... to ... go!"

'Fortune', I admitted, meant minor acclaim by way of a published letter in *Xenoarchaeology Quarterly*, followed by a lengthy scientific paper. But that was enough for a position in a university in some peripheral system, or maybe even toward the center of the spiral arm.

Cold practicality intervened, shunted the flow of enthusiasm into storage. How to prove this, then, without a record? Perhaps, I thought, just a *little* more recording. I'd have to catch the Curator at it, of course; I'd have to wait.

"What you say, Squigs?" I turned to the Curator. "One more…"

"Welcome."

What was I saying? What was I thinking? Already twice, I'd rebuked myself for cruelty, committed to do no evil. And here I was, planning yet another round of villainy.

I could make notes. Record my own impressions. Dictate my comments. That would get me no more than an excerpt in the Letters section of some minor journal. Which would draw one or two real xenoarchs, who would make recordings. They'd get all the glory. And the Curator would get the anguish — the same unhappiness I was trying to spare it, or worse.

Back to step one then — I might as well do it myself. I'd done it before. I could do it again.

It would be harder this time, though. In the last few hours, I'd somehow come to think of the Curator less as 'creepy old creature' and more as 'charming, enduring companion'. It was beautiful, it was ancient, and it only wanted one thing, "no images".

Two things, perhaps. Maybe three. It wanted to welcome others, it wanted to scratch on the altar, and it wanted no record made. No visual record. Why?

I went back outside, slid a statipack from my thigh pocket, and settled down to a lunch of fermented pola nuts and thought. I reached no conclusions and didn't taste the food, but I made a decision.

"Squiggly," I said, stepping back into the temple.

"Welcome."

"Welcome," I agreed. "I want to test something, okay?"

"Welcome."

"Promise not to get angry?" I held out a hand, gripped a tentacle lightly. It twitched, but didn't pull away. It was firm, but surprisingly delicate. Not really well suited to wire gripping. I looked closer, and soon spotted a pale spot on one of the other tentacles. The Curator shifted form, but perhaps it had a preferred rest setting, a default, with a spot that was callused or raw from holding the little wire. Or maybe it was just a freckle. It didn't matter.

I let loose the tentacle. It flapped about a bit, then settled into the same slow wave as the others, like a cat's tail that's been held and then set free.

I stepped over to the altar. As I'd thought, there were two jagged scratches on it. Ragged, raw, and obvious now that I knew to look for them, one like an angled S, the other like a crooked Y. They hadn't been there on the images from previous expeditions. The altar's carvings had been studied near to death, and there was no way they would not have been noted.

"Here we go," I warned, taking up my first metal spatula. Lightly, as lightly as possible, I traced the second scratch, the Y. The Curator twitched, but didn't move, didn't speak. I traced it again, with a little pressure now on the tip of the spatula.

"Welcome."

"Welcome indeed." It seemed a good sign. A promising start. I traced the scratch again, pressing much harder now. If I did this enough times, my theory went, I could win the Curator's trust, and it would let me make a recording or two. It entered my mind that I was, without a doubt, contaminating the field, but I let that go. One step at a time.

"Welcome," the Curator said, each time I traced the scratch. Little by little, grain by tiny grain, a fine, powdery dust accumulated in the scratch.

"Well, then," I said, as I stretched my back, and worked the cramp out of tired fingers. "So far so good." The Curator said nothing, but it looked to be a brighter, more vivid shade of yellow. Of course, I'd been in a dimmish temple for some time now.

"Let's try the other one, shall we?" I stepped around to the original scratch, as I thought of it, the one shaped vaguely like an S. It was deeper than the other, when measuring depth in fractions of a millimeter. I set my metal stylus on it, traced it out.

"No image," said the Curator.

I stopped. This was a setback, without doubt. Ten minutes of steady "welcome", and now we were back to "no image" already. The Curator was a fickle creature.

There were no signs of anger or outrage, no green flush. The yellow petals pulsed steadily in spirals around the trunk. I traced the scratch again.

"No image."

No other reaction. It had done the same, I realized, the other day. The exact same.

I traced the scratch again.

"No image."

And again.

"No image."

Harder, this time.

"No image." The spirals ran faster, but they were all yellow, and the petals fluttered freely.

It had to be. I traced the Y scratch again.

"Welcome."

I traced the S with shaky hands.

"No image."

Back and forth, back and forth until there could be no doubt, though mine had long since gone.

Y scratch — "Welcome." S scratch — "No image."

I set down the spatula, left it on the altar.

"Squiggly, my boy, you are something else." But what?

I thought about it all the rest of the day, sitting with my back against the temple, the Curator standing friendly by my side, every now and then letting out a tuneful "Welcome". I thought about it that night, over a statipack of something or other edible. I thought about it until I fell reluctantly asleep, thought about it when

I woke up in the middle of the night, and as I dressed in the morning.

"Squigs," I said, as I stood once more in the entry of the temple, and it flowed back to let me in, "the way I see it, we have three possibilities.

"One. You're making those scratches as a reminder of the only things you have left; maybe the only ones you ever had. One for welcome, one for no image. Maybe you're a guard dog, maybe you're a degenerate sage, maybe you're a rocktree that's slowly learning new tricks. But you know your memory's not so hot, and you're setting your two favorite phrases down in stone. Maybe you remember the builders doing that, or maybe you were inspired by these carvings." I waved at the altar. "Who knows how old you are?"

"Two. You're renewing your programming. You're — no offense — some kind of elaborate cyborg or genetic robot, and out of desperation, you've taken to trying to fix up your own circuit board. Only," I waved again at the altar and the scratches, "you don't have quite the same artistic touch as your makers." I looked again. The scratches were definitely deeper now. The spatula was ...

over in the corner, next to the now-redundant piece of wire.

"Three. Something else. I admit, that's by far the biggest category, but I don't want you to go wild with it. And I admit, one and two aren't really all that different. But there's a difference of intent, I think; an important one.

"Thing is, Squig, there's a test we can do, that might help us find out." The Curator stood silent. "What do you say we try?" It went well against my xenoarch training, but that seemed to have gone by the wayside in the excitement, with only the faintest of squeals from my conscience.

I went over to the corner of the temple, picked up the spatula, came back to the altar. I studied it carefully, as I'd studied the oldest records all morning. I positioned myself perpendicular to the doorway, to get the most contrast on the altar, then flicked an overlay up onto one lens. I set it to auto-adjust for perspective, waited until it had settled and run a range of precalculations for possible shifts in position.

"Here we go, buddy." The Curator was across the altar and to my left. With as delicate a touch as I could master, I set spatula to stone. I'd chosen the shortest, simplest curve that I could still make out, and the clearest, oldest record I could match to it. Softly, I ran my spatula along it, with one eye on the altar, one on the transparency, and a third, if I'd had it, on the Curator.

Nothing happened.

I stood up, looked the being over carefully. Was the yellow a little more orange? Were the spirals going the other way? I closed my eyes, couldn't remember. It was hard to see color in this light.

I stooped again, ran the spatula carefully over the curve. Again and again, slowly, until I was certain I was getting it right. There was definitely a tinge of orange now, and the petals were spread flat against the trunk, except when they swirled in complex patterns of spirals and circles. It was very pretty.

"We are getting somewhere, Squigs!" I pressed harder, staying as close to the true path as I possibly could. My arm knew the movement by now, and I was confident I was fairly close. Two more runs, pressing harder every time, until the Curator, now a vivid apricot, broke out into a ululating, earsplitting cry of screeching, crumbling lumber mixed with bird calls and the sound of thunder. It wasn't pretty at all.

I dropped the spatula and ran. I stopped halfway to the ship; my usual spot. When I turned back, the party was over. The Curator wasn't visible, and I jogged slowly back, tacking toward the forest to maintain my distance from the entry while getting a view into the temple.

The Curator was bent over the area I'd been tracing, slowly feeling the surface with one tentacle, dragging the spatula along behind with the two others. It was trying to etch it deeper!

I stepped closer, and the being immediately stopped. "Welcome," it said, holding out the spatula.

I took it, stepped cautiously back. Those tentacles could grip, that was clear enough, and there were enough of them that the Curator could hold me with no trouble. No more trouble now than yesterday, or the day before.

"In for a penny," I offered, and stepped up to the altar.

The Curator had done a terrible job. The new scratches were jittery and angular, where the original etching had been smooth and sinuous. The new scratches ran the risk of completely obscuring the old. Already, I had trouble seeing where my marks had been, and where the new ones went wrong. If this was reprogramming, it was going to lead to some serious glitches.

"No scratching," I said, gathering up the spatula and the discarded wire. "You don't have the eye for it."

Actually, I realized, the Curator had no eyes at all. Clearly it could sense things; it sensed my presence well enough. But there didn't seem to be any actual light-gathering apparatus. "Pretty good for a blind … thing," I amended. "But not good enough. Not to do restoration work."

My own skills weren't good enough either, I realized. It was one thing to test a theory. It was another to rewire a stone circuit board, or whatever this was. Who knew what might happen? The Curator might not be deft, but it looked to be plenty strong. More than strong enough to throw me against a wall, if I triggered the wrong subroutine. A bit like sticking electrodes into a man's brain, really. Run some voltage here, his left arm raises. Run some there, he recites Nuaji poetry. Over here and …

"Run some there and he recites Nuaji poetry," I repeated, as a chill settled on my shoulders and worked its way down my breasts. I backed slowly out the door, spatula and wire carefully in hand.

I backed up to a safe distance, halfway to the forest. It might be a safe distance. Who knew?

I remembered my first day on the ground. I'd seen the temple from the side, the Curator's slim yellow tentacles flickering in and out of the entry. Like a tongue. A long, yellow, very, very forked tongue.

I'd stood there next to it, reached out my hand to hold it. Standing in the creature's very maw. What else could it be? If that was the tongue, the entry was the mouth. And mouths don't only speak.

I shuddered. How close had I been to disaster? No wonder it said "welcome". The next phrase was "come into my parlour", no doubt.

I slept poorly that night, locked behind a sealed port with the manual override engaged, and a makeshift barrier outside my berth. I'd been in the beast's mouth, perhaps its belly. Jonah had nothing on me, except perhaps a certain amount of style, and a lot of divine backing.

Only one thing kept me from flying out of there as soon as my hands stopped shaking enough to activate the controls. The Curator said "welcome". Logical enough, if you're a huge stone flytrap with a prehensile tongue. Got to get the suckers in somehow.

It also said "no image". Where was the sense in that? "Step right up, make yourself at home while I make you dinner. Oh, by the way, no pictures." Your average mass murderer, human sacrificer, wants a little recognition. Your average carnivore couldn't care less. Why the stricture against records? What difference could it make once the victim was in the trap? For that matter, why hadn't it eaten me already? Or any other expedition in the past twenty thousand years?

Twenty thousand years is a very long time to be patient. It's also a very long time not to eat, even if you're a rock-based organism. If the thing had forgotten how to eat, it would be dead by now. Instead, it was very patiently, and very badly, performing brain surgery on itself with its tongue and a piece of wire.

The curse of the scientist is in not being able to let go. We're like detectives and like cats in that, except that cats have more lives, and detectives have armchairs, and sometimes guns. I'd have like to have something behind me, even if just a chair. The nearest thing to a gun was the ship, which was hard to carry around. I settled instead on a recorder. Maybe all it would do was anger the thing, but at least it would be a distraction.

In slow, careful stages, I walked halfway to the temple. The skull. The being. Whatever. 'Temple' seemed silly now, but it was the best I had. Besides, heads had temples, didn't they? Two apiece. There should be another around.

"Get a grip on yourself, woman." Hilarity and hysteria were far too close together to risk confusing them now.

I walked halfway again. And another half, until I was only a few meters from the structure.

"Welcome," said the tongue.

"Yeah, sure."

"Welcome."

"You would say that." This was getting us nowhere.

If it did eat, where were the bones of its kill? Yet if it were photosynthetic, why would it need a tongue? Even if the tongue were more for talking than for taking, whom would it talk with? Why would it need to? And why to humans? In all the novels, thinking mountains thought very very slowly. How... Or maybe that was why. Maybe the tongue was semi-independent. Maybe even, and this seemed quite likely, part of some sort of symbiotic relationship, and not technically part of the temple at all. Of course, then both of them would need to eat. Best not to think of that.

Still, why the prohibition on recording? How did it even know? Obviously it had senses I did not, but my recorders were purely passive, receiving light and sound as they arrived. How could it sense such a thing?

The best way to find out, it seemed to me, was to ask.

I'd spent the morning well away from the temple, setting up a complete record of all my thoughts, all my data, and all my speculations. I attached the recordings I'd made, cross-reference with all the files I'd brought. I even mentioned the dust — both kinds, loose and solid, and how the loose kind had led me to my discovery. I set out in detail the steps I indented to take. When I was done, I sealed up the ship, squared my shoulders, and marched to meet my doom.

It felt like doom. I had my recorder, and I'd brought my finest stylus, a sturdy durasteel probe used for testing masonry in the finest of building cracks. It was cheap, but it was tough.

"Right, then, Squigs." The phrase was missing the camaraderie of our earlier exchanges, but I was aiming for bravado instead. "Brain surgery 101. Pay attention."

I'd like to say I stepped bravely into the lions' den, but in fact, I slunk in on shaky legs, keeping my back to the wall. For all I knew, the wall was where the giant stone teeth were waiting to grind me into altar paste.

Methodically, I traced line after line as well as I could, starting with the clearest. I traced and traced each one with just the faintest touch, until the movement felt natural, until the software said I was staying within a one percent margin. It wasn't great, for brain surgery, but then I wasn't a brain surgeon. Not by training. I didn't touch the pattern I'd used the other day. Whether through my own carelessness or through design, if one can say that about synapses, the result had been frightening; I didn't care to chance it again. When taking stupid chances, it seemed to me, it might pay best to take ones not *known* to be dangerous.

When I thought I had ten of them down, and when the Curator — the Curatongue? — hadn't yet thrown me to the teeth, I started back on the first. When I'd traced it five times again within my margin of error, I increased the pressure. The first firm tracing did nothing. Nor the second, nor the third. The scritching, scratching grind of the stylus started to wear at me. I didn't dare look away from my work, but I could tell that the Curator was close. Four times, five, with no result, and I stepped away. Sweat drenched my back and plastered my hair to my forehead. My shoulders were so tight they hurt.

As I stepped back, the Curator flowed forward. I scrambled back, heedless of stone teeth until the temple wall was cold against my back. Yellow-pink tentacles traced across the path of my stylus, the thin scratch I'd managed.

"Welcome!" it boomed.

I shut my eyes. Volume control. Or enthusiasmotor, or adrenalith gland, or some other outlandish thing. Not speech.

"Welcome," the Curator said in a more normal tone. It had flowed back to its normal place, across the altar from me. Pink spirals chased each other around its trunk, and its petals danced in intricate patterns. Not helpful.

I did line two. No result. Line three. Line four. Line five. Each led to different displays from the tongue buds, different colours, different arrangements of tentacles. It was lovely, elegant, and utterly unrelated to Common speech in any form I or my analyzers could recognize.

I took a break after five. It wasn't surprising, really. What were the chances I'd hit the right combination out of the who knew how many that must be available? The oldest records hinted at layers and layers of lines, at different depths. And that was just the surface. Who knew what mineral nerves lay within the altar, and what had caused them to stop working? A scratch on the surface was just that — a superficial mark that could mar but not effect real change.

I ate a snack. My shoulders were tightening already from tension, and that wouldn't help. I stretched doggedly until the muscles loosened as much as they were likely to.

"Okay, Squiggly." He stood in his place by the altar, tentacles wrapped into an intricate basket at waist level. Like a seat. "Thanks anyway, buddy. Not yet." I went back to my usual place, across from him, the altar safely between us.

Line six. Line seven. Line …

"Thank you."

I raised my head, only for my neck to spasm painfully. Warm tentacles helped me lurch upright, held me while blood rushed to my head and stars danced before me.

"What was that?" I squinted across the altar, trying desperately to refocus on a distance further than ten centimeters away.

"Thank you." The tentacles let go. "Thank you for your help."

It talked. For real. Full sentences and everything. "Um. Sure." Just what I'd wanted. Why I tried to recall? Why had I wanted it to talk? I'd had a question, surely. A question.

"What do you eat?" I blurted. That had been it. The grip of the stylus cut painfully into my hand. I'd feared the answer, this morning.

"People."

My shoulders sagged. That was it, then. I dropped the stylus. What was the point? I'd never fight this thing. Probably the stone mouth was already shutting, the teeth emerging. But I had my answer. I clung to that, wrapping my arms around my chest as the shivers started. Relief, I thought.

"You have the humor?" the Curator asked. "You are a species with humor, with jokes? This is a joke."

"You're telling me." How many meals teach their predators to speak? That was a joke if I'd ever heard one. "Don't talk with your mouth full." That was another.

"I eat the ... essence..." Oh, it got worse? Wonderful. "The companionship, the company."

"Just get it over with already. I'm the only company you've got. Start sucking up my essence or let me loose."

"I have already done so."

I frowned, looked down at my body. I felt like myself. I looked like myself.

Essentially and otherwise. Uncrumpled, unmasticated.

"I don't get it." Here I was, prey for a brain damaged vampire rock skull, and I didn't even understand it. Bad xenoarch.

"I feed on on companionship, on the presence of others. It does them no harm, I believe. Some even enjoy it."

Not many enjoy being fed on, in my experience. Maybe there was supposed to be some kind of gaseous emission at work, but if so, I didn't feel particularly calm.

"This is the reason for the Squiggly," the Squiggly said. "You call it the Squiggly? Or Squigs? The Curator. The Interlocutor. Interlocutor is best." It wriggled shyly, and a violet pattern chased across all the tentacles before disappearing into the trunk. "It is to entertain, to caress, to nourish, to solicit, to speak."

I looked at it. At the Interlocutor, anyway. I wasn't even sure just what I was talking to yet.

"So Squiggly calls them in, and you feast on their emissions, is that it?" Like one of those fish with a light on its head. Glow, glow, snap.

"Yes. But with no harm. And some benefit. The Squiggly can feed you, if you desire." The Interlocutor proffered a long tentacle, now dripping with some clear yellow fluid.

I shuddered. "No, thanks. I had breakfast." A thought came to me. "So what does Squiggly eat, then?"

"It eats me." I knew there was a catch. "Sunshine, minerals. I draw them up from the soil, from the rain."

"For twenty thousand years?"

"When I run out, I make changes." I remembered the upheavals in the land surrounding the temple, the rises and falls of land.

"You did that? The lake, the cliff, the ridge?" The ridge was a good kilometer away.

"Yes."

"So what do you eat when there are no people?" As there had not been for a decade.

"Animals will suffice when needed. The Squiggly is very versatile. It can welcome many types. My minimal needs are small."

"So then, what happened?" I gestured to the altar, unsure now whether the Interlocutor could see me. "How did your brain get … this way?" I eased away from 'erased'.

"No image," squawked the Interlocutor immediately. "Yes, 'no image'," it repeated in a more thoughtful tone. "I feed on companionship, respect. Conversely, I … wither … in disregard. 'Feeding' is a simple but inaccurate term. Perhaps it is better to say that sympathetic, pleasant interaction generates brainwaves that resonate with my own, build their amplitude, allow me to manipulate my own form in addition to the land around me. Analytic, dispassionate, distant interaction generates waves that dampen my own, that cause my control to … lapse. When that happens, my systems degrade, my structures slump. As when visitors make recordings, rather than using their own senses. You see the result."

I looked down at the altar, with its faint lines, its painstakingly scratched surface, and at the skirt of dust at its base.

"Dust!" I gasped. "The dust." I'd been right after all. Sort of.

"Yes. The dust. It remains part of me, but disordered, chaotic." The Interlocutor chuckled. "You re-established my language capacity, in a rather brutal way."

"Hey!" Here I'd just done delicate brain surgery on a stone-brained twenty thousand year old alien, and it was complaining?

"Oh, I appreciate it. You did better than the Interlocutor could. And perhaps the day will come when I can reestablish the circuits properly."

"What do you mean?" It was talking, wasn't it? And I was here! "Feed away."

The Interlocutor waved its tentacles. "Much as I savor your ... feedback, it is a crumb to the feast I would need." It paused. "Can you bring more people?"

"What? No." Not in my tiny ship. And yet... "How old are you?"

"Old, even for my kind, though we are few and far between. One million local years. Perhaps a bit less."

A long time. "So you've met other races. Talked with them."

"Oh yes."

"And you remember." I looked back at the altar with its tracery of faded, failed synapses.

"Mostly. The efferent systems are the first to go. Memories are stored elsewhere."

"I have an idea."

So that's why I'm in sales now. Sure, I've got a dozen honorary degrees or so. Mostly, though, I run the SI Center for Advanced Xenoarchaeology Research. No recorders allowed.

I get in touch with distinguished xenoarchs who are a little past their prime. People with big names at big universities, but without much new to say. They come and ask the Interlocutor questions about past spacefaring civilizations that have visited. Then they go away and write groundbreaking articles as 'thought experiments'. It's amazing how often supporting evidence turns up, once you know where to look.

We invite the names to give lectures on our lovely grounds. They stand on the top of the temple and speak to huge crowds of attentive, companionable people. The dust is already disappearing from the base of the temple walls, flowing back in to reestablish the simpler neural pathways. Humans are very useful, Squiggly says, and easily influenced. I feel like that line of thinking should bother me. Maybe it would have before. I suppose that's the drawback of living with a giant stone brain. Maybe some of its ways are starting to rub off on me. Still, I wonder whose idea it was to start calling the brain an altar, and why we still do.

See B. Morris Allen's story "Graven Image" online at Metaphorosis.
If you liked it, leave a comment. Authors love that!
Remember to subscribe to our e-mail updates so you'll know when new stories are posted.

About the story

Some stories come all at once, and some come in stages. "Graven Image" was one of the latter. I can't remember why, but I wanted to write a story about frottage — the technique of creating a design by placing paper over an image and rubbing a colored substance on it — perhaps familiar to some from grave-rubbing. I combined that with the idea of a ship coming to a lonely planet. The visitor, I thought, might come away with a slightly different image on each visit. I still might write that story, but somehow this one found its way to alien temple carvings — indecipherable, of course. From there, it was a short step to the idea that tourism would literally kill the spirit of the place, and that the temple was an actual creature. The details changed a little as the piece moved on, but that was the genesis. I toyed with alternative titles, including "Frottage" and "Hold that Thought".

The Yarnball Woman

Michael Milne

By the third time Patricia lost a finger, everyone knew better than to raise a fuss.

Her family hadn't always been this calm. When the first finger, a knuckle's-worth of her left pinky, had fallen plumply into her dinner salad, there had been an enormous commotion. Her young daughters screamed and bolted into the back yard, and hours later had to be coaxed back inside. Jack fumbled with the phone in the kitchen, trying to maintain an even voice while holding back tears. The family border collie, Bernard, stationed himself next to Patricia, barking at the table and the fallen digit. All the while, Patricia sat staring at her dinner and her finger, unable to move, as though crying or sealing herself in the bathroom would invite some new calamity, allow new seams to loosen and more body parts to shake free.

This finger disassembled like the others, severing just below the nailbed. June, the elder daughter, hadn't noticed anything, but Leila was looking and let out a calm, plaintive sigh, like the sound of a pillow being fluffed. Whatever form her exclamation had wanted to take, Leila snuffed it and formed it into something tamer. *The girls don't want to embarrass me*, Patricia thought. She dreaded that they were already burying their own feelings on her behalf.

She had just painted her nails in aquamarine, and the tiny nub lay lifeless on the hardwood like a dead scarab. There was no blood and no wound, just a smooth, curved tip. Like it hadn't come from Patricia at all.

"Do you want this, Mom?" June asked, gesturing towards the table. She had a tight smile plastered on her face, though Patricia could see her eyes growing wet.

"Yes," Patricia said. She found herself relieved she hadn't lost a forefinger—

which would have made it harder to operate a camera—and then surprised that relief was the first emotion past the finish line. "I'll need to keep it fresh." Would she feel something else later, when the family doctor sternly shook her head, and carted the piece of her away in a miniature medical waste receptacle?

Patricia's daughters were still young enough to take cues from their parents—they could get used to anything. They knew to get bags and ice, to stay calm. They knew not to call for an ambulance. None of their actions would save the finger, of course, but the action plan seemed to comfort them. And Jack, too.

"Should I order Leila and me a pizza?" June inquired. Leila had scurried to the backyard, notifying her father, and then moved upstairs without another word. Both June and her mother pretended not to hear the door slam, or the sobbing.

This nonchalance they all tag-teamed was a form of pre-grief, though she would never call it that to her family. When the first chunk of a finger had lopped itself off, when she had withdrawn a foot from her boot two toes lighter than before, the family had been devastated. They had tried fad diets together, sat in the offices of countless baffled specialists. Jack was starting to dabble in more woo-woo cures, and they could barely find shelves for all the new crystals they owned.

But along with it all, Patricia detected a growing, polite acceptance, like a bed of mushrooms sprouting in the expanding dark. In the absence of a recognizable disease, the comforting burden of a sharply defined prognosis, Patricia's tendency to lose pieces of herself was growing to seem like a quirk of her personality than a calamity.

"I'll make an appointment, Patty. An hour's wait at the most." Jack had entered from the backyard, scanning the room and offering a decisive nod. He squeezed Patricia's shoulder once, and then went to get the phone. Without any exposed nerves or vessels to actually use for replantation, Dr. Liu tended to pessimistically refer Patricia straight to specialists and prosthetic makers. But calling the doctor was part of the ritual, part of the routine. Jack took pride in his duty and care, especially when the alternative was so much screaming and crying.

Patricia permitted herself to join in optimism. She didn't think that the crystals or all of the amputation triage would do any good, but she was still confident that the doctors would one day stop her body parts from falling off.

After a few years of dedicated collecting, Patricia decided to give up on the headscarves. She had amassed quite the array, fine silks and cottons in a mass of patterns. Sabine, who ran the hijab shop at the strip mall down the road, had taught her a dozen ways to tie and drape. Sabine called her "Mrs. Patricia" and was comfortingly discreet, teaching her how to pad and mimic a full head of hair below the fabric.

But Patricia had heard too many questions behind her, so many strangers misfiring and artlessly explaining cancer to their children. She recalled her own grandmother—her daughter Leila's namesake—withering away to breast cancer, her floral headscarves a blaring siren of her disease. Patricia decided she couldn't be brave anymore.

"You look beautiful, my sweet. New hairdo?" Jack, bless him, did not even seem to blink at the wig. She had aimed for incognito: a boring and frumpy brunette style, almost exactly the same colour and shape she had worn before clumps of her own hair started coming loose. She had brought old pictures of herself to the wig shop.

"Just got back from the stylist," Patricia said. She was relieved that they could joke, that if Jack had questions, he was restraining them.

"Modern fashion!" Jack said. "Maybe I should get something new?" He ruffled his own hair, then came to kiss his wife on the cheek.

Jack left it there, and Patricia was thankful. He went about preparing dinner —they'd all gone raw vegan—and Patricia ignored the quiet sigh she heard from the kitchen. As Patricia sat and read, her hand sought out the ends of her new hair to play with, a forgotten habit she took joy in reclaiming.

Later that night, she would set up her camera to take a picture to send to June. Older now, both girls were much better at dealing with Patricia's condition. But June lived away from home, and never had to find misplaced toes forgotten in the bathroom.

"I liked the wraps better," Leila said, returning from school, her weighty backpack heaved onto the couch beside where Patricia read.

"I liked having hair better," Patricia said. Leila recoiled, and Patricia was left to wonder how acidly she had said it. She had lost the ability to gauge her tone, and that had been messy with two teenage daughters. "Sorry. Sorry, honey. I'm just sick of explaining that it's not chemo." Though for a while cancer had been a nicer excuse than a bewildered shrug. "Besides, now you can grow your hair out!"

Months before, when the first curl of Patricia's chestnut hair had snarled in the collar of her pea coat, Leila had caught it. Without saying anything, she had withdrawn a pin from her purse, drawn her mother's hair back, and covered the missing patch. As more hair fell, as Leila began sculpting with less and less clay, she had done her own hair to match her mother's. And when that became too much, Leila walked her mother into Sabine's and shaved her own head the next day.

Leila drew her hand up to her head, ran her fingers through her closely cropped hair. She wore a pair of Patricia's earrings, which glinted and swayed in the negative space framing her head.

"I think I'll keep it like this. It feels lighter."

"We won't match anymore," Patricia joked. She hoped she made her voice sound light and airy.

"I'll keep matching you, mommy." Oh God, she was crying. Had Patricia sobbed without meaning to? "Even if you don't always match yourself."

When June requested the engagement shoot, Patricia couldn't resist. She would make the best of things.

While Patricia didn't take many commissions or shoots anymore, she still liked the idea of adding to her personal collection of photographs. With both girls out of the house now, Patricia had no one to drive her during the day. She would clamber awkwardly onto the subway and slowly make her way across town on her two canes, pausing occasionally to slowly pull the viewfinder before her eyes. She still kept a dozen business cards in her purse—*Patricia   Anne   Atkinson,*

Professional Photographer—but felt too embarrassed to give them to anyone. Every venture out was increasingly awkward and difficult, tinged with the growing sense that it might be her last opportunity to use her camera.

Leila took most of the actual engagement shots, under her mother's direct command. Her daughter had a knack for photography, and Patricia had been trying to cultivate it. Together they had decided on simplicity, a pleasantly decrepit gazebo in the nearby park, and a luckily sunny afternoon. The fiancé called her Mrs. Atkinson all day, overtly formal, and glanced away whenever she struggled with her canes. Patricia was too excited by the photo shoot to find this annoying.

"Increase contrast by five per cent," Patricia told her computer. "Turn off that blue auto-filter!" She'd need the girls to review the pictures anyway. She could no longer see the colour red, and she tended to oversaturate her photos to compensate.

Her adaptive laptop had a variety of assistive apps, including the photo editor in which she now worked. They had gone for an all-purpose device, as her disabilities changed by the day and had no predictable course. Or explanation. For now, she could still manipulate the mouse with her remaining half-fingers, though some of the voice commands intuited her tone enough to get the gist of what she wanted. Occasionally the computer would take too many liberties, would assume her wants and add hideous hues or start playing classical music in the background of her work.

"Crop and frame. A touch left. Now rotate maybe three degrees clockwise." A shot taken from up near the rafters, where Leila had scurried, both Patricia and June's fiancé giving her a boost. She had giggled hard enough to miff the angle, but the smiles made the shot too good to delete. "There. Perfect."

"That's a lovely picture," Jack said from behind her shoulder. He often checked in on her when she was working, as Patricia was wont to shout the computer down when it couldn't interpret her commands. "Really, Patty. I think June is thrilled you're doing these."

Well, it's mostly Leila, Patricia thought but didn't say. He brought her a glass of water and held it at straw distance while Patricia slurped, not making eye contact, as though to afford her a sliver of dignity. The water probably contained one one-millionth of boiled down moonwart or vervain, knowing Jack. Unconvinced by mystical healing, she had decided to find his efforts loving and tender.

Right now, though, she felt only resentment that Jack had to hold the glass for her, or Leila the camera. They were middlemen, though she was still the photographer, the water-drinker. But when would her involvement become tangential enough to go uncounted, her joys conjugated exclusively in past tense?

Jack watched for a time, but left as Patricia fell silent in her work. She came across a few photos she had taken herself —with Leila supporting her arm, bracing her. After the loss of the first round of knuckles, Patricia's fingers had continued to shrink until she could barely hold the camera. Now, she could tell all of her shots were blurred, and she deleted them.

The last in the set had been taken by the fiancé, what-was-his-name... Ted! Patricia smiled at a portrait with both girls flanking their mother. They held her up, but their support looked casual, serene. June had just told a joke, and all three women were caught mid-laugh, their matching blue eyes gazing at one another.

"Computer, remove..." but Patricia stopped. There was an autoblur at the creases of her prosthetics, the synthetic and natural skin blending in. Adjusted lighting and the breeze made her wig look suddenly realistic. Patricia paused, hovered over the controls. With a few clicks she shaved off years, removed the straps of her prostheses, all evidence of her medical shunts. She looked, in many ways, like the woman she had been a few years before.

Patricia hated herself for a moment for being so vain, but she decided to keep the picture as a sort of reminder, as a goal. Jack had started a Vision Board, and he would be touched if she pretended at interest.

A deep part of her felt, in a way she didn't care to address or name, that this was the way she wanted to be remembered. That after she was gone, this was the vision to be stamped into memories. She sent the picture to her daughters, saving a copy for herself.

She woke up one day as normal, stretching her arms and the hand-with-some-fingers high above her head. In her bedroom with Jack, she went without her prostheses, but she always tried to dress and en-limb herself before she confronted the world. With so many pieces scattered around her nightstand, the carpet, or rolled under the bed, reassembling herself took a few minutes. Jack had not stirred, and so she tried to muffle her grunts, frustrated with each finicky clasp and strap. All the while she imagined deliberately planting a plastic hand in the grocery store, or abandoning an ear in a restaurant bathroom, just to give some cooing, pitying stranger a scare.

Her wheelchair, parked just along her side of the bed, was cold against her skin as she hauled herself into it. After nearly a year of practice and dozens of pounds of lost weight, she performed the manoeuvre in silence. The controls to her chair were difficult to operate with so few fingers, but she found herself too proud to switch to a puff-and-sip model. At last she was composed, a simulacrum vision of herself, ready to set sail in her chair for the day.

It was still dark in the kitchen, the sun just rising out the windows. In the quiet she put on the coffee, feeling satisfied that she was part of the familial routine, and settled herself at the table to read.

It wasn't until breakfast that she noticed what was gone.

"Morning, Jack." She had the newspaper spread before her, paperweights on the corners.

"Morning." Her husband smiled at her for a minute, his mouth working back and forth like he was chewing gum. "Good morning." And then again the chewing.

In truth, neither of them could properly grasp the problem until she rolled to the front door for the mail. Bills, wedding invitations, touch-activated holographic coupons. All of them addressed to Jack Atkinson &

They all trailed off that way, the gulf beside the ampersand expanding like a white sea with no horizon. The woman felt an emotion stir inside, and after struggling to name it, she decided it was loss.

Jack finally cottoned on and began sobbing. He called Father Schwarz, the latest guru he'd turned to for advice and answers. In the backyard, the woman could hear Jack trying to curtail his tears as he described the problem.

"Hey Ma, what's up?" Leila was back at home for the summer before her final year at university. She glanced to the backyard and spotted Jack. "What happened?"

"It's nothing, dear. I need some help writing a few emails to the lawyer. Do you think you could help?" Her computer, though skilled at voice-to-text, had difficulty transcribing her speech. She had lost her /s/ and /l/, and Leila was much better at interpreting her words.

She kept things vague, as Leila didn't need to know the gritty details of estate law or power of attorney. She made sure to ask after Mr. Attakar's children and wife, and insisted Leila include something about the weather or the news.

"Perfect, dear. I'll sign it and send it."

Leila, accustomed to being her mother's scribe, squinted at her. She tapped a few keys and screwed up her face with curiosity.

"Oh." Leila's mother wasn't so good with masking her feelings anymore, and Leila approached for a hug. They tried all of the variations of her name; even the initials were gone. Leila's fingers would work, but get tangled; or the keystrokes would produce nothing on the screen. At best, she could type "Mr. and Mrs. Jack

Atkinson" but both women prickled at the anachronism.

"I've got an idea," Leila said. She signed the email from herself with her full name, Leila Anne Atkinson, on behalf of her mother. "You picked out my name, right? Family names or something."

It was a wedding, or some other big fancy event. The woman couldn't tell, but Jack laid out an elegant dress for her, one that mimicked volume and covered her legs. She watched him get dressed, and remembered feeling attraction to him—not the comforting love she still held, but lust and want. As he dressed, she tried to simply enjoy the way his limbs still moved in concert, the dextrous way he pulled a belt around his waist.

"When did you get that tattoo?" she asked.

"A few months ago. At half Christmas." She had lost her birthday years ago, and they celebrated her now in mid-June. He leaned over so she could see the ink across his shoulder.

"A man of your age with a tattoo," she cawed. Jack smiled, as though they had done this before. "It looks like somebody's hand print."

When Jack was dressed, Leila Anne came up into the room to help her mother. The process was arduous, with a dozen criss-crossing harnesses across her torso. The dress Jack had picked was long and dull: any colour too flashy would make her look even stranger, as a few weeks previous she herself had gone black and white.

"You look smashing, Ma. Even better than at my wedding!" Leila Anne smiled, and the woman tried to remember when her daughter had gotten married or to whom. Leila Anne positioned her parents in the foyer and took a few pictures, promising her mother they would look classy in grayscale.

The event was fine. Though bereft of much to think about, she was able to tune out most of the religious content and enjoy the stained glass on the windows. Churches bored her, and she was sick of being dragged to so many of them, of people praying over her. When they went to the reception, however, things became too complicated for her to navigate.

The guests at their table, ones the woman felt certain she either knew or was required to know, whispered incessantly. They watched her as she ate, which was a messy and difficult process, and she had lost the ability to taste much these days anyway. They watched as she talked, which was also messy, though Jack and the girls rarely let her feel it. They watched as she watched, seemingly certain that she wasn't aware of them.

The men and women of table 12 cast piteous glances at her, and talked to Jack about her in the third person. Had they ever figured out what had happened? Was it, they said only half-jokingly, some sort of curse? When they made painstaking efforts to include her in the conversation, they talked as though she were a child. If she had the fingers to tensely grip the sides of her chair, she knew she would be squeezing with all of her might.

"Are you having a good time? This is a really delicious meal, isn't it?"

"It tastes like shit," she said. She said it a few more times when the others couldn't make out her speech, and at last Jack interpreted for her. No amount of façade would impress people. No one would even pretend she was the same as she once was.

When the woman was home at last home, and Jack had settled for a quiet whiskey after positioning her in their bedroom, she sat before the mirror for a long time. She considered her hands: how little of them was left, how much was plastic, and whether she would ever recall their original shape. How much she wore for herself, and how much she put on so she wouldn't disturb others.

She thought of all the blessed herbs and fluids positioned around the room, on her chair, under her pillow. She gazed at her eyes in the mirror—once, someone had said one of the girls had her eyes, but now they were a cloudy grey. She consulted a nearby photograph of herself and the girls to confirm that her eyes might once have been blue.

With a steadying breath, the woman loosened the first strap. Her fingers had lost their finesse and so the harnesses with extra buckles and bands were the most difficult. When the last clasp loosened, the thighs decoupled in a sweaty gasp, and the woman felt lighter.

She let lengths of fabric and padded leather fall to the ground around her, draped across so much shaped and grey-pink simulated skin. And she decided it would be the last time she wore any of it.

The man carried the woman around in his arms as he went about their morning routine. In the pale light seeping through the windows, she was just able to make out what he was doing. Her vision was still sharp, though she found it difficult to make sense of what she saw.

The man made them both breakfast, and she noted the pains he took to make it taste good. By necessity it had to be all liquid, but she never had need to complain about the flavour.

The quiet of the house was occasionally broken by the shuffling and sniffling of the animal. She wasn't sure the name of this one, and cute as she found it, she felt sure it wasn't the one she was used to. Unable to really fend off dogs, the woman was often placed quite high in different rooms.

"Trisha's here," the man said to the woman. She liked Trisha, though she found it hard to place exactly how they were related. She looked like someone that the woman knew; those eyes.

"Hi Grandma," the girl said. Yes! That was it. "You ready to go the park?" The woman couldn't reply, but she could smile, and that was enough.

Her wheelchair was soft and insulated, with steadying straps on each side. The girl, Trisha was her name, could capably lift the woman into it without assistance. They wheeled through the front door, down the ramp, and into the crisp afternoon.

The woman liked these trips to the park, though she sometimes found them difficult to deal with. She would remember sometimes, short recollections of herself and the man, frayed snippets she couldn't grasp the ends of. Walking, using her long legs, pushing a wheeled vehicle herself, some smiling pink lump held within. Was the lump now this girl, Trisha? It seemed too long ago, and Trisha herself too young. She remembered wearing dresses, colours picked to match her eyes or the season, and she remembered pulling them on herself. She remembered sitting in the park with the man and some animal, tossing a drool-soaked tennis ball into the brush, the animal very small and the woman's stomach very large.

They came to a bench, and the girl parked the chair before coming to sit alongside the woman. They could not hold hands, and so the girl placed her arm along the hand-rest and leaned close.

Wrapped in a long, heavy scarf, the girl looked familiar. The woman searched through the people she knew, trying to place her. Was she her child? A niece? A girl from the neighbourhood? It was the eyes, the woman decided. Those blue eyes shone from a face she couldn't recall, like they were on loan.

"Do you like this scarf, Grandma?" the girl said. She must have caught the woman staring. "Mom told me it was one of yours. She said you would probably be okay if I wore it."

Yes, yes, she said to herself. Whatever she didn't use anymore, she was happy for someone else to wear. She had closets of clothes, she had seen them this morning, all too big, too bright. It would be nice for someone else to wear them.

The girl eventually withdrew a slim camera from her bag, affixed a heavy cylinder to its front and began taking aim around them. She stood and crouched and moved around, always within arms' reach of the chair. Whenever she seemed satisfied with her shot, she would coo, observe it in the viewfinder, then lean back from her position to show the woman.

How beautiful, the woman wanted to say to the girl. The colours and the what-was-it-called, the ratio, were just right. She wondered who had taught this girl to shoot, to frame. She watched the girl photograph the autumn scene before them, and tried once more to remember the girl's name.

See Michael Milne's story "The Yarnball
Woman" online at Metaphorosis.
If you liked it, leave a comment. Authors love
that!
Remember to subscribe to our e-mail updates so
you'll know when new stories are posted.

About the story

"The Yarnball Woman" came to me after lots of discussions about dementia with a close friend. Her own mother was going through early onset dementia, and I had just finished a university course on the psychology of aging. My friend talked about the pieces of her mother which were long gone, and how much more she seemed to lose than her memory. At the same time, I was reviewing course videos of patients with Alzheimer's, and watching how they confronted the strange losses in their lives.

The story first formed as a middle-aged woman who began to fall apart, quite literally. I imagined her fraying over the span of a few scenes, with fingers and toes disappearing, and then with more fabulist and strange losses as the story goes on. I had considered leaning harder into the parallel with dementia and memory loss, but as Patricia started to fall to pieces I realized there was already plenty to play with. She has to confront her loss of mobility, her increasingly challenged relationships with her family, her ability to engage with her hobbies and her profession.

As it becomes clear that her condition is irreversible, she and her family try to find ways to preserve her, either physically or in memory. Her daughters and her husband have to fend off their own grief for a person who, while changed, is still alive. Meanwhile Patricia herself has to mourn the pieces of her that go missing, while not always knowing what she has lost.

A question for the author

Q: What's the story no one else thinks is as good as you do?

A: "She Waits, Seething, Blooming" by Dave Eggers is a perfect capsule of a story. It is the thinnest sliver a short story can be, a perfectly defined cross-section of a character's life. It's so, so good because it's so, so short: the story itself is complete, and has a definite arc over its tiny wordcount. But it contains multitudes, and you can absolutely sense the world before the story takes place and the world after. We never learn the main character's name, nor her son's, but we get such a perfectly shaped glimpse of her life that we don't need to. I remember reading this story years ago and suddenly being convinced of what short fiction can do, and I reread it (it doesn't take long to read again) a few times a year when I need to edit!

About the author

Michael Milne is a writer and teacher living in Switzerland. He has written speculative fiction and overstayed his welcome in coffee shops throughout Canada, China, Korea, and most of continental Europe.

www.michaelmilne.ca, @ironcardigan

Familiar in Her Angles

E.A. Brenner

The trees in this part of the Dragonwood are thin and lanky, like growing boys, like her own willowy limbs, but Lina has no interest in the trees, or young men, or the body that conveys her, stomping feet falling where they will. Her thoughts are for the great lizards, those remote majestic beasts sunning themselves on the high rocks jutting from the tree line. She looks up to patches of hot blue sky through the canopy of green leaves far above. Her feet are bare. It is the hottest part of the day, and everyone else is resting in the stone-coolness of the house. Around Lina the air is thick, dark, and green, sitting on her skin, sinking into her hair to run down her neck in rivulets. Every time a twig or stone digs into the sole of her foot, her heart leaps. *Soon,* she tells herself. *Soon. Please.*

She pauses her stomping to lift her hair against a light breeze. Heavy and thick as her arm, the braid falls to her feet and even a little beyond, dragging on the ground, pulling her head back until her scalp aches. Strands escape constantly, wispy things flying about her face. She wishes she could cut it off, pluck the hairs from her head, shave down to smooth unburdened scalp like her grandfather, like widows and oracles, bald beneath wimples. If her aching scalp were bald as a dragon's egg, she would throw the bones and divine her own path, be reborn from that egg and fly away with the dragons. But she cannot—Lina is not an oracle, a widow, an old man, or a great lizard. She is not free to do as she pleases. Lina was bought from a witch, on the promise that her hair remain unshorn. Lina was seen by the oracles as the wife for the Prince. She will marry him in a week's time, and become not only a wife and a princess but her family's greatest honor. The Prince's tower looms in the distance, beyond the

Dragonwood. No matter which direction she walks, the tower grows closer.

Six months ago, the oracles came to their village, descended on the family estate, declared Lina the match for the Prince. They had seen it. "The desired outcome," they said as they sprinkled herbs in the fire and tied knots in thread pulled from Lina's clothes and bedding. They circled her beneath the full moon and smoked an owl pellet. The stink turned Lina's stomach and lingered in her hair for days. Over the shoulders of the oracles, she watched her mother and father clutch hands, eyes bright in the smoke haze. This was the sum of all their hopes and dreams.

Little Lina was already a miracle child when the oracles arrived, hoped for and prayed for, sacrificed for on the feast days and saints' days, and finally, when all else failed, paid for from a witch, a wandering oracle cast from the circle of the sisterhood. For Lina's mother, no more watching as her sisters-in-law dropped baby after baby, strong boys and girls, while her arms remained empty. Just a little hedge magic, a little twist of fate, a promise, and Lina came squalling into the clan of the wolf. That night, her mother likes to tell the story, the moon was in the constellation of the Tower, the sun in the Queen's throne. "The gods laid this path for you in the stars," her mother repeats over and over as they stitch her trousseau, tiny stars on the borders of towers and wolves' heads. "Your stars will make you a queen, my little Lina."

While no one is looking, Lina stitches her stars in the constellation of the dragon.

The royal household descends three days before the wedding like skeins of geese pausing their migration, raising a village of silk tents on the western lawns. Lina and Prince Ector are introduced. Ector's eyes are brown with flecks of gold and green, like dragon skin. They are warm and kind, but guarded.

They stare silently at each other, strangers shy of getting acquainted. Lina is more interested in speaking with Ector's cousin, the Duchess Honoria of Felchess, whose travelogue of her tour through the far eastern Dragonwood Lina has read four times. Honoria sits several tables away, waving a wineglass in the air to punctuate her storytelling. She is probably regaling the table with her account of the buffoonish tour guide who didn't know the difference between a male dragon and a nesting mother, whereas the Duchess, being well-read in the authorities on the subject, corrected the poor young man for the benefit of the tour group. Or perhaps she is not speaking of dragons at all, but only some court gossip to titillate her audience. Lina looks away, down at her own wineglass, in which she sees the distorted reflection of her hands, fingers curled into strange pale claws. She reaches toward the reflection and wraps familiar fingers around smooth glass.

Their families' murmurs grow edged with concern as Lina and Ector eat their first meal together in silence.

The evening is claimed by the women of the house, who brush her long hair, scrub calluses from her feet, hands, elbows, rub perfumed oil into her skin, share their secrets. She has been happily on the giving end of this exchange for many of the women in the room, but now that she receives these attentions, she finds the ritual an imposition. She doesn't want smooth skin and smooth hair. She wants scales and claws and fire. She wants to be a dragon. Some days she can almost feel the shape of it beneath her skin, an itch of dissatisfaction, subtle and patient.

A year ago, while brushing her cousin Caenis's hair in preparation for her wedding, Lina quietly voiced her discomfort with the idea that someday she would marry a man, not because she disliked men or marriage, but because she did not see herself as a wife, or some days even a woman.

"Are you two-spirited?" Caenis asked

"No," Lina replied, wishing then she hadn't said anything, wishing she could take it back, as the other women around them paused their conversation and listened. "I don't want to be a man, or live as one, or marry a woman."

"What do you want, then?" her mother asked. It was a gentle question, not a challenge, but Lina shrank away, suddenly uncertain of what to say. Wishing to be a dragon meant turning her back on these women, separating herself from them, from her whole family. She didn't want them to misunderstand, to believe she wanted to be something else because she thought so little of them and what they were. That wasn't it at all, but she had no words to express the itch inside her bones.

Now, as then, the room is pleasantly warm and full of family. Caenis brushes Lina's hair and whispers their favorite story in her ear: the tale of the unhappy princess who demands her suitors bring her the tail-tip spine of a dragon, but the would-be husbands must procure that needle-thin spike without killing the beast, an impossible task. Lina stretches out long and languid like a dragon on the midday rocks, lets Caenis's voice break against her like water as she turns her attention inward and questions her desire for the thousand-thousandth time. For weeks after her confession, Caenis and her mother questioned Lina about it, but she avoided answering. When the oracles arrived and declared Lina a match for Ector, everyone seemed to breathe a sigh of relief that said *well, there's Lina's answer. Now she won't be confused anymore, and we can all stop worrying about her.* But she is still confused. The oracles' pronouncement did not settle her mind; it only created more turmoil. Lina believes in the power of the oracles to guide people to the best path, but her desire to be a dragon has not been quelled. Nor has it settled into the kind of certitude that would allow her to say, "the oracles are wrong."

It is rare, but there are stories of people who defy the oracles. To do so requires a level of confidence in oneself that Lina does not possess. She has never been anything other than herself, and every other day, she wonders if her desires will change, worries that becoming something else will not settle her uncertainties at all, worries she will make the wrong choice if it is ever hers to make.

Her family celebrates her impending transformation into wife and princess long into the night, but the thought of becoming either stirs no emotion other than regret that the transformation she truly wants is fading into an impossibility. Her questions will never be answered.

The household sleeps the morning away and convenes at midday for another meal.

Ector brings a book to the table and sets it down between them. Lina catches the Queen's pinched look of dismay, but it is forgotten when she looks down and sees her copy of Jaffo's *A History of the Dragonwoods*. She knows it is her copy because the pages are marked with clumsily-embroidered ribbons from her childhood.

"I found this in the library," Ector taps the book with a long slender finger. "The marginalia look like your handwriting." He pauses, and when she doesn't respond, he adds, "Perhaps I should have waited until after the meal?"

"It's my book," Lina finds her voice on the other side of her surprise. "Have you read it before?"

Ector nods enthusiastically and ignores his food. "Three times! I searched the royal archives for a year looking for evidence to support Sir Rampion of Hunstead's claims about the offspring of the dragon and the wyrm, but no accounts of his Caravan of Marvels noted a single sighting. Does your family archive hold anything?"

Disappointing him feels like kicking a puppy, but Lina shakes her head and says, "No, neither our archive nor the neighboring estates have any accounts to verify Hunstead's claims. We do, however, have generations of observational studies of the dragons' mating seasons to show that his claims are specious. The dragons don't mate with the wyrms and wyverns, nor do they eat them."

To her surprise, Ector doesn't look disappointed by her revelations at all. "Fantastic!" He exclaims with his voice and his hands, and almost knocks over the water jug. "I didn't know the estates here kept records of the mating seasons. Do you think they'd send copies if I asked?"

"I think they'd send you anything you asked for." Lina puts a grape in her mouth before she states the obvious. He's the crown prince. He has only to ask and he receives everything, including the best-suited wife. Is *this* why the oracles saw her as the ideal match? They both love dragons? Her enjoyment of their conversation turns to dust in her mouth, and she swallows the urge to gag on the grape. She will spend her life talking about dragons with this man, and never be one.

Ector is too busy flipping to a page covered in her scribbled notes to notice her distress. She swallows some water and answers his questions with a smile. He asks for a tour of the woods in the afternoon, and she agrees.

There is a heated argument amongst Ector, his guards, and his parents when Lina arrives at his tent for their afternoon walk. The rest hour is over, and the heat of the day has gone down, but Lina has missed her opportunity to walk barefoot and alone. For this walk, she'll have to keep to the path with her shoes on her feet. If, that is, Ector is allowed to go into the woods at all.

"—dangers!" a guard bellows.

"The dragons don't attack people, and they certainly don't eat them," Ector rolls his eyes. "It's well documented—"

"Forgive me, your Highness," another guard interrupts, "but not everything you read in books is true."

"He'll be safe." Lina steps into the tent, into the circle of wary faces. "I go walking in the woods nearly every day. No one here has ever come to harm unprovoked."

Ector looks to his parents triumphantly. "My lady will make sure I am unharmed."

The Queen rolls her eyes, and Lina stifles a smile at the sight. Ector takes more after his mother than his father. "Oh, fine," the Queen huffs. "But take Honoria with you. And your guards."

Between Ector's questions and Honoria's questions and stories, two pleasant hours pass and Lina talks herself hoarse. No, dragons on this end of the wood are no wilder or tamer than the dragons on the other end of the wood. They mostly eat wild boar, mountain goats, and antelope, but occasionally snatch up sheep that wander from the herd. They bury their dead and mourn them, like the elephants in the lands to the south. There is an account in the library from a hiker who came upon the dragon's graveyard in a hidden valley in the central mountain passes. Lina promises to show the diary to Ector when they return.

They keep to path. They return safe from possible harm.

In the library, Lina leads Ector to the corner she claims for herself. All the books and folios about dragons line the shelves between the window and the fireplace, all within easy reach of a cozy armchair. While Ector's back is turned and he exclaims over her collection—"I stopped looking when I found Jaffo on the chair there this morning! If I'd seen all this I never would have made it to lunch!"—she plucks shed strands of her hair, so very long, from the chair's back and drops them to the floor.

Half a dozen times, she has sat in this chair and held a blade to her hair, sick of the burden, and half a dozen times her hand has been stayed by the intensity of her parents' fear. The hedge witch did not say what would happen if Lina's hair were cut, but her parents imagine fearsome consequences and have never allowed more than an inch to be trimmed from the day she was born. She loves her parents and dreads disappointing them more than she hates her hair, more than she distrusts a disgraced oracle's soothsaying; this is the only thing about herself she never questions.

Beside the fireplace is a mirror. Lina comes here to be alone and look at her own face, sometimes for hours, studying each angle, curve, line, and freckle for some sign of who she is, and whom she might become. Some days, her face seems that of a stranger looking back at her. Some days, she covers the mirror with a shroud, ill from her longings, wishing them away. Two years before, she tried giving up dragons, stayed away from the library for weeks, until she was so empty she lay in bed and wished for death. But the feeling was not strong enough to kill her, so she disdained it, got out of bed, and started walking the woods barefoot, seeking a different fate.

The diary she hands Ector contains not only an eerie description of a valley full of dragon bones, but also the clearest account she's ever read of a dragon spine and its properties: a slender needle-like growth fifteen to twenty centimeters in length jutting from the very tip of a dragon's tail, perhaps the vestigial remains of armored spikes spanning the backbone, now easily broken off or, the diarist theorizes, shed and regrown annually like a deer's antlers. Sharp enough at the tip to penetrate the flesh of a mammal. All accounts of the consequences of a dragon spine penetrating the flesh are unverified, old wives' tales of men made into monsters; no one in living memory can speak to the possibilities of a dragon spine. Unfanciful naturalists posit that the spines are not from dragons, but from some plant in the Dragonwood, and caution that they are likely poisonous, given the descriptions of their unnatural effects on the flesh.

In the middle of the night she returns to the forest, abandons the path, abandons her slippers in the undergrowth. She hopes for a dragon spine with every twig and pebble pressed to the soles of her feet, but her feet remain pristine. Even the dirt doesn't stick.

In the darkness, the Tower looms.

She can't say no. In two days she will marry the Prince. She will become a princess, the stuff of stories, but she yearns to be something from a different story. As soon as the oracles gave their pronouncement, her mother stopped asking what Lina desired. Before Lina grew accustomed to the strange question, her opportunity to answer it was gone. The words of witches and oracles determine her fate. The night grows warm, and she grows warmer from the fury rushing through her. When has she ever had a choice in who she is? Her hand falls to the knife at her waist, a ceremonial gift bestowed upon her at dinner. She must wear it through the next two days, to symbolically sever her ties to her family so she can be bound to another. Ironic, that fear of separating from her family has stilled her tongue for all this time, has stayed her hand from severing her hair, has wrapped her desires in doubt. Her fingers grip the hilt.

When has she ever felt brave enough to make a choice? When has she ever done more than leave it to chance?

Lina stands still in the forest, and the rage fades away, leaving an echoing chasm of doubt and regret and longing in her chest. If she refuses this marriage, her family will be ruined. Her forays in the forest are coming to an end, and so too her chance to go toward the thing she wants instead of away from what she doesn't. Every turn she takes, the Tower follows.

Her head aches from the heat and the weight of her braid, and she wonders for the thousandth time why the witch didn't say what would happen if she cut it off, only made her parents promise to let it grow and grow and grow. They have all been so afraid, so fettered by it, unable to see beyond it. Dragon or princess, neither gives one whit for the length of her hair. Perhaps she cannot choose the transformation, but she can choose to be unafraid of who she becomes. Lina draws the knife from her belt, steel so fine and sharp it hums in the sudden small breeze created by its movement. She lifts her braid, cuts it, and drops it to the forest floor, light-headed for the first time in her life.

Her mother flies into a terrified rage when she sees what Lina's knife strokes have wrought and must be calmed with fortified wine.

Ector compliments the close crop. "It brings out your lovely eyes," he says. "Doesn't she look fey, mother?" He smiles, and she sees his sense of humor hiding in the corner of his mouth. "Soon, all the ladies of the court will shear their tresses from envy."

Lina's mother looks so relieved she might pass out. The queen looks like she is trying very hard not to roll her eyes again. Ector insists Lina will become the muse for every court artist, the inspiration for every painting, the object of every swain's poem.

"It's more comfortable in the heat of the day," is all Lina says. Her mother glares at her, silent instruction to move along to a different topic of conversation, one that does not involve her deep streak of pragmatism in the face of romantic gestures. "I love to walk in the sun," Lina reveals, feeling petulant. Then she recalls that she intended to reveal nothing more of herself. She does not want to encourage Ector, even though she knows the conclusion is inevitable and she may as well make the best of it. But Lina is not the sort of person who makes the best of things. She came into the world with grasping hands, as her mother tells the tale, although Lina wonders where this desperate grasping person is hiding. She does not know her.

The prince smiles and agrees. "I love the heat here. It sinks into the bones. It can grow cold in the Tower." He holds her hands loosely, not limp, just loose. His grasp is easy and confident, his fingers warm and dry. His nails are neatly trimmed. Everything about him is neatly trimmed. He changes the subject and asks her if she believes that dragons shed their spines and grow new ones like deer and their antlers, as the diary-writer speculated, or if she thinks a dragon has only one spine for life. She can't see anything hiding in the corner of his smile now. Through the window over his shoulder, she sees a lone dragon fly above the forest, unusual in the heat of the day when they rest in the mountain caves and sun themselves on the rocky slopes, and her heart aches to join it.

They lock Lina in her room after the noonday meal, but she climbs out the window and down into the Dragonwood. She walks for hours in the heat of the afternoon, reveling in the breeze on her neck, the strange weightlessness. When she returns, her feet are clean, and her parents are sitting on her bed waiting for her.

They confiscate her rope, confiscate all the rope they can find throughout the household and even from their royal guests, and when they put her to bed that night, her father locks the windows from the outside. It doesn't matter. The wedding is the next day. Her fate is upon her. She lies sleepless and stares at the stars, sticky and listless in the oppressive air of the closed room, the warm night pressing against the glass.

She finally drifts into a strange state of quasi-sleep when a rock crashes through her window. The glass shatters, and the crash startles her to her feet. Picking her way over broken shards, she trips on a lumpy bundle, lost in the murk of the floor. Fumbling, she closes her fingers around it and draws the thing up close to her face to see it in the moonlight: a silky roughness wrapped around a chunk of stone.

The wrapping falls away in her hands, glides between her fingers. It is a rope. Pale, thick as her thumb, tightly braided. The silk running through it is familiar in her hands, a twining of colors in the strongest fiber, for she used it to decorate and bind her now discarded braid. The rope is crafted of her own hair.

Footsteps sound in the passageway outside her chamber; voices echo against the walls.

She doesn't stop to think. Instead, she unlocks the window and scales the outer wall, heart pounding every time her feet slip. The rope, hastily secured to the bed, holds. The house awakens beneath her, lights flaring, windows and doors heaving open. She reaches the ground and runs to the Dragonwood as her family calls after her in the darkness. It is middle night, when the dragons roam.

Without hesitation, she enters the wood.

The pain when her foot finds a spine in the darkness is so great she cannot stop herself from crying out. The trees absorb her screams, their dead leaves cradle her as she falls to the ground. The spine has pierced her foot, emerging through the top. She waits five agonizing minutes, counting the seconds with whimpers of pain, before drawing it out. She needs to be sure it will take. Blood runs thick over her fingers. The pain is a fire running up her leg. Her foot has gone numb. She wipes the spine clean and weaves it into the side seam of her nightdress, desperate with hope that it is the right kind of spine, that the tales are true, or, if they are not and she has failed, that it is poisonous and she is dead by morning because this pain is too much to bear for nothing.

Ector finds her sitting with her back to a tree, binding her foot with strips from the hem of her nightdress. He is gentle, pressing the torch into her bloody hands so he can carry her. "Did you find what you were looking for?" he asks. Flickering torchlight illuminates pieces of sympathy on his face. Nearby, loud voices and the bays of hunting hounds echo in the forest.

"I don't know," she replies, burying her face in his cool neck. She can feel her fever rising. "It's too late anyway."

They dunk her in cold water to bring down the fever, wrap the foot so tightly her toes remain numb, but nothing stops the fire in her blood. She sweats through three nightgowns until finally, at dawn, the shaking stops and she feels almost cool in the light of the rising sun. She sleeps for an hour, until they wake her to bathe and don her wedding gown. Her mother hides Lina's shorn head beneath a veil heavy with decorations and presents her to the Prince. He looks well rested, and she wonders if she dreamed him finding her in the forest.

The ceremony is traditional, except that the oracles officiate, a very rare boon.

Lina and Ector are handfasted. They feed each other the bitter greens and the sweet, kneel and speak the ancient words. Over their heads the Oracles chant the binding spells. Most people forego the spells these days (none of Lina's cousins married under magic), but the royal house keeps the old ways.

Lina swallows panic in deep gulps at the thought that the binding magic might interfere with the work of the dragon's spine. Although she has no way of knowing if she's succeeded except waiting, she refuses to give up hope, even on her wedding altar, even as Ector looks at her, so pleased. He judders as she does, when the binding flows between them, a prickling suffusing the limbs, starting in her hand where it touches his, tracing up her arm, over her shoulder, and down into her chest to wrap around her heart. Pain flares in her foot, white hot. She gasps. Around them, the onlookers gasp with her, thinking they are witnessing one tremendous thing, when in fact it is another, all unknown to them. As she loses awareness of her body, feeling only the fire consuming her foot, she is glad she has this for herself.

The wedding party lasts all day and well into the night. The fire in Lina's foot is the only thing keeping her awake enough to grit her teeth and smile at the endless guests. She is surrounded by people, but loneliness rises within her. She is so weary, she feels removed from her body and her thoughts. Lina watches her mother and the Queen speak with the oracles. What did the queen sacrifice for the oracles' insights about her son? What did Lina's mother sacrifice to bear her? What is Lina sacrificing to change the course of her own life? One of the oracles catches her staring. They regard each other across the distance and the fading light, until the oracle smiles knowingly and winks. Confused, Lina turns away.

Ector—her husband—takes her hand. His fingers are long and cool. He waits for her to grip.

When she does, his smile is so brilliant it catches attention and a cheer goes up around them. She is caught between feeling secure and feeling lost. She wonders if the dragon spine is real, if it took, or if she is just nervous and fevered and married. He looks happy.

He leads her to a chair tucked in the corner of a garden hedge away from the crush of people. A flick of his wrist, a gesture, and three guards appear to stand perimeter around them, holding the guests at bay. A young boy brings a tray of food, a pitcher of water, and a carafe of good dark wine. While she eats for the first time in over a day, he confesses in a low voice, as though he had reached inside her and found her thoughts, "I believed I would feel different. They told me I would feel more settled after the binding, but I still feel restless. I want to see the Dragonwood again. I've never been there until yesterday." He doesn't comment on his participation in her midnight excursion. His voice is wistful as he continues, "I've wanted to visit so many times, since I was a small boy, but it was never permitted. And once we leave here, I doubt I will have the chance again. Is it silly that I hoped to meet a dragon, and charm it into giving me a spine?"

Lina reaches for more wine. It quenches her thirst, but not the heat in her belly. " 'Why do you court me?' the Princess demanded." She quotes the story

Ector has referenced, her favorite story, and waits for his response. Does he know it as well as she, as well as he seems to know everything else she loves?

Ector smiles. "To see you happy," he quotes the bard's response. The bard, who of all the princess's suitors brought her what she demanded: a true dragon's spine, from a live dragon. "For every time I have passed through your court, you have been borne down by a great sadness. I would see you free of it. I ask nothing in return but to write songs of your joy."

Lina finishes the tale: "The princess took the spine from his hands, and to the astonishment of her court, plunged it into her own heart. Instantly she was enveloped in flames, and when the flames died out, a great dragon curled around the princess's throne, for she *had been* borne down, by the curse of a wicked witch, transformed from a dragon queen into a human princess, trapped while her dragon clan suffered her absence. Freed by the bard, she returned to her clan, who rejoiced to be reunited with her. They granted the bard the boon of a hoard, but he did not retire to become a landed baron as people expected. He remained true to his declaration and traveled many countries singing songs of the dragon queen's joy."

Ector drinks his own wine. "Alas, I have no dragon's spine for you." He leans close. "I wanted to issue a decree that I would only marry a woman who could bring me the spine of a dragon. My mother went to great lengths to dissuade me, and in the end had to consult the oracles to make me see reason." He shows her humor, but there is a longing in his eyes, etched into the angles of his face.

Lina's attention is diverted as, one by one, the guards turn inward to face them. The fire in her foot flares. Beyond the guards, the crowd presses in. The garden corner shrinks. Faces peer at them over the shoulders of the guards. They are on display.

Ector's shoulders stiffen, and his face composes into a pleasant, somewhat vacant expression. She understands then, for the first time, that they share a cage. "The spines are just a story," she lies. His face falls, just a fraction, and she is surprised that she can read him so clearly when they are barely acquainted. Her heart breaks a little. She fingers the hem of her veil, where she has hidden the used spine, ready to confess her lie and give him this small gift in recompense for the trouble she might soon cause, but the Prince stands to meet his obligations and she is carried along with him, because they are her obligations now, too.

She didn't expect to love him. It makes this much harder.

The newlyweds are given a suite of rooms near the top of the Tower. Their daily complaints about climbing the many stairs become their first shared jest, because they would not trade their rooms for anything. The view of the forests is unmatched. In the morning and the evening, they watch the dragons spiral and swoop over the woods, hands clasped. They make love on the balcony, matching their cries to the screams of the dragons in the distance, and Lina has never felt so present and comfortable in her own body. It is a strange revelation, after so long contemplating what else it might be, but it does not settle her old discontent, and the tension makes her as restless as ever.

Ector was right about the cold at the top of the Tower, but the heat grows inside of her, stretching her, pushing its way out. She orders cold baths, sometimes three times a day. She feels hungry and faint and her thirst cannot be quenched by water or by wine. Her mother-in-law and the ladies of the court whisper of babies behind their hands and a hopeful anticipation fills the Tower.

Ector seems not to notice her heated skin, her agitation. He seems content, no longer the caged bird. Lina feels betrayed. She thought he understood, but he smiles and goes about the business of preparing to be king someday with purpose and drive. He speaks of all the things he is setting in order for the future but does not speak of the Dragonwood, even as they begin and end their days by watching the dragons.

Lina doubts everything. Perhaps there is no transformation coming. Perhaps her foot was pierced by an ordinary thorn. Perhaps she is simply overwrought with nerves and conflicting thoughts to the point of fever. Her husband makes her laugh, and doesn't tell her she is too much or too little, and would it be so bad, really, to live out her days with him? He is an ideal partner, and she is torn between a good man and a desire so entrenched she cannot open her hands to let it go.

"Don't worry, dear," the queen pats her hand and mistakes her restlessness for other desires. "A child or two will draw you down to the ground." Her head feels heavy, as though her braid yet weighs her down.

On the day Lina singes her clothing simply by putting it on, her doubts fall away and she knows her time is coming. The heat and the pain are unbearable. She weeps, and even the cold of the mountain that blows past the Tower as the season turns brings her no relief. In spite of it all, her heart lifts in anticipation, then plummets with guilt when Ector looks her in the eye and smiles.

She tries to send him away, but he refuses to leave the room. He turns away visitors, barricades the door against his guard, and burns his hands to blisters holding her.

"I'm sorry," she cries. "I didn't mean for it to happen this way."

"Shhh," he kisses her hair, smooths the short length grown during their brief marriage. "You're perfect. This is perfect. I won't leave your side."

The transformation steals her breath. Bones melt in a fire and settle into new shapes. Hair and cloth burst into flames, filling the room with an acrid stench that does not smell to her the way it had to her old self. She is tangentially aware of pounding at the door, questions shouted, her own screams going on and on and on. Ector holds her gaze with his warm gold-flecked, dragon-skin eyes, doesn't flinch, not even once. In their short time together, she has only begun to plumb the depths of his endurance, the extent of his stoicism.

She thought she would grow larger, but she stays the same size, only rearranged. Perhaps, she thinks, she will grow as she ages. For a dragon, she's quite young.

She has wings now, and a long tail.

She breaths fire from her snout.

The room is very quiet.

Ector looks different to her new eyes. She can see the sadness in him, colored threads of blue and pearly gray. There are also patches of red and orange—excitement. "Marvelous," he breathes out, and then asks, "Can you understand me?" She tries to nod, a strange movement with such a long neck, and her body unbalances. Her new tail gets away from her, knocks over a table, topples a vase to the floor. The shards of pottery remind her of shards of glass, her window broken so mysteriously.

As though he knows her thoughts, he says, "I threw that stone at your window. I found your hair in the wood and made the rope, because suddenly there wasn't any to be had. I was hoping you'd find a spine." His face stretches into a vast, unabashed smile, and he lights up with a joy colored purple and yellow like pansies in sunshine.

Lina draws her tail around; it obeys her this time and goes where she directs. Her new limbs feel as natural as the old. There at the tip of her tail is the thing they both desired, a desire so strong it found its way into the stars and brought them together, from a hedge witch's baffling charge that Lina's hair remain uncut to the sly matchmaking of the oracles, everything intersecting to produce their desired outcome.

"May I?" he asks. She masters a nod and nudges him with her snout. Her love for him swells in her with an unexpected fierceness, and she wonders if all her feelings will be magnified into this heady, exciting wine of emotion sliding through her belly. There is no pain when he snaps the spine from her tail. He meets her gaze and, without hesitation, plunges the spine into his thigh. Like Lina in the forest, he cannot stop his scream of agony.

The door bursts open with a mighty crash, and the king and queen, half a dozen soldiers, and the court physician pour into the room. There are shrieks and cries at the sight of her, and Ector urges her toward the balcony. "Go!" he urges. He cannot stand on his leg—the spine remains very deep in the flesh. Soldiers raise swords and advance on her, but they halt as the Prince throws up one hand to ward them off. He pushes her with the other, balancing against her to hold himself up even as he tries to thrust her away. "Go!" he shouts over the din. "I'll find you!"

She pauses in the balcony doors. Evening has come. In the distance, the dragons begin their descent from the mountain peaks into the woods. They call out over the land, and a reply rises from her belly, tears from her throat. It echoes over the valley, and one by one, the great dragons turn to answer her. They circle in the sky, draw closer to the Tower, beckon her to join them.

She looks back to him one final time, and in the reflection of the glass balcony doors, she sees herself transformed, sleek and strange, yet familiar in her angles and her oldest imaginings. He says again, "I'll find you," and draws the spine from his leg, holding it aloft in triumph. When they meet again, he, too, will be altered yet familiar.

She launches herself from the Tower, rises on powerful wings, and takes flight.

See E.A. Brenner's story "Familiar in Her Angles" online at Metaphorosis.
If you liked it, leave a comment. Authors love that!
Remember to subscribe to our e-mail updates so you'll know when new stories are posted.

About the story

In the summer of 2015, I read Angel Carter's *The Bloody Chamber and Other Stories* for the first time, and the first draft of "Familiar in Her Angles" popped out. I struggle to write short stories, so I was surprised how quickly that first draft came, amazed I managed to get from start to finish in only a few pages. I was reading a lot of fairy-tale retellings and fairy-tale theory that year, so when I realized I was playing with the motifs of the maiden in the tower fairy tale (Rapunzel, Petrosinella, Persinette), I leaned into it.

Through several drafts I looked for ways to subvert the roles and tropes and also explore how we build and embrace our own identities. Also, I needed to write at least one dragon story in my life.

A question for the author

Q: What's an idea you're dying to write but haven't, and why?

A: An idea I've been dying to write is a Mission Impossible-style magical thriller. I adore over-the-top spy movies and magic-in-modern-times fantasy. I haven't even started such a story yet because I don't have a character or plot to hang the genre on. I'm waiting for the day my main character drives through my mind in an incredibly sexy muscle car and orders me to get in.

About the author

Elizabeth Brenner grew up in Toledo, Ohio and moved to Boston, Massachusetts to get an MFA from Emerson College. She loves hardware stores, making jam, stories about magic spilling everywhere, crochet, travel, and smart jokes. She makes a living as a managing editor for scholarly journals and is a member of the Boston Speculative Fiction writing group. She lives with her husband in Salem, MA.

Combustion

Kai Hudson

Jaxon has just finished doodling Captain Fiero's victory pose when the math teacher explodes.

Students scream as Mrs. Richardson flails back from the chalkboard, body suddenly alight. Her arms and legs make a bright windmill as she stumbles across the room, upsetting the fake plastic skeleton and catching the bookcase on fire. Jaxon shoots to his feet without thinking, grabs his jacket, and runs to her just as she collapses across Hannah's desk.

He's too late. Jaxon stands there staring as Mrs. Richardson's body jerks and twitches, the fire finishing its meal. The room fills with the stink of burnt hair and cooking flesh.

There's no time to mourn. With a high-pitched wail, Robyn catches fire across the room. Adrian rears back from her and turns to run—he lights before he gets two steps away. Order collapses. Children shriek and cry and dash for the exits, while the fire leaps from one tiny body to the next, Jaxon darting after it with his jacket flapping in futility. Smoke burns his eyes and clogs his throat, everywhere ash and heat and flame. Finally, he stumbles out of the classroom alone, coughing and retching as he scrubs flecks of classmates from his eyes.

Around him, the world burns.

He presses the jacket to his mouth and nose, staggers through thick smoke and lashing flames. A couple times he hears something like screams coming from a nearby room, but when he turns to run in —he'll save them, Captain Fiero would— all he sees is fire. Greedy orange tongues that speak in hisses and pops: *Come sit with us. Come here where it is warm.*

The school's front doorknob sears his palm. Jaxon yells and shoves forward, tumbling down the steps and into soft dirt.

He lies there and breathes, sucking in deep lungfuls of air that tingle and scratch on their way down. He keeps at it even though it hurts, because that's what Captain Fiero would do. Captain Fiero would breathe, and slowly push himself up to sitting, and go out to save the world.

When he sits up, the city is on fire.

Flames spew through broken-glass storefronts. Cars drift aimlessly into each other, their drivers on fire. Two blocks down, the old church lights the afternoon, huge flaming pillars punching out windows to grasp for the sky. Everywhere fire, everywhere death. What—what is going *on?*

A high-pitched scream, and he turns. A woman runs down the sidewalk, arms flailing. Smoke pours from her clothes and her whole head is aflame, a meteor with legs. She falls to the ground just as Jaxon reaches her and throws his jacket over her head, holding his breath to keep the smoke out as her body seizes and trembles beneath his. After a second he remembers to hit the jacket with his palms like the people do on TV, and the lady gives one last heave before going still.

The parts of her arms and legs that aren't charred and crusting around bone are pale and scattered with freckles like only white folks have.

He holds the jacket down for a while longer, just in case the fire comes back. But though his palm still smarts from the hot doorknob, the heat seeping up through the thin cloth doesn't feel new. Jaxon takes a deep breath and lifts the jacket.

The fabric peels up with chunks of scalp, skull, and sooty hair stuck to it. Beneath, the lady's brain glistens grey and dead in the bright sunlight, like a new flavor of Jell-O Nana might serve for dessert.

Sickness punches up his throat. Jaxon turns and spews his lunch all over the asphalt. His hands shake as he drops the jacket.

Which is when something roars.

He looks up to see a monster approaching in the shape of a white van, flames shooting out its grill and from beneath the hood. It bears down on him, only feet away, and Jaxon stares. He wants to run but can't. He can only think stupidly, *This is gonna hurt.*

Then something hits him from the side. The world flips and he finds himself staring up at clear blue sky.

Strange, he thinks, that the smoke from a thousand burning souls can waft up into that great, endless unknown and simply disappear.

The man who saved him looks nothing like Captain Fiero. He doesn't wear a bright red cape with yellow flames at the bottom, or surf through the air on a fireball he makes from his hands. Arthur —"Call me Artie, son"—wears a shirt with sweat stains at the armpits, and thick jeans that look like they've been washed about a thousand times, the blue all sucked out of them.

He was in the Navy before, something called a core-man. Artie says that means he looked after people when they went out to sea or into the desert and got shot by the enemy. Jaxon wants to ask if Artie ever met Donte, if maybe he'd known Jaxon's brother before he got blown up in Iraq and came home in a flag-draped box. He can never seem to form the question, though. Donte's death is its own little hurt, like even now a part of Jaxon's heart is continuously burning sharp and acrid.

It's not the only thing still burning. Down below the mountain, the city continues to smolder, thin columns of smoke and ash drifting up from the charred husks of buildings. Two weeks have passed since everything went up in flames. The radio stations squawk nonstop, experts and analysts and counter-experts and counter-analysts all picking and pulling and voicing their theories, but to Jaxon their panicked conversations sound like water circling a clogged drain: motion without progress. They keep saying what a big tragedy this is and how everyone needs to work together to do something about it. Underneath it, though, Jaxon only hears fear. Fear, and relief that it didn't happen to them.

There are conflicting reports about the spread of the destruction. Some stations describe whole countries consumed by fire, reduced to nothing but a wasteland of embers and ash like in the videogames Donte used to play. Others claim it's just a few cities here and there, Jaxon's included. No matter what the reports say, though, everyone agrees on two things.

One: the fire keeps spreading, fast and unpredictable, a few people suddenly lighting up in the middle of the day for no reason and subsequently taking an entire city down with them. And two: no one knows why.

They could probably figure out that second one if everyone just came together, pooled their resources and ideas to try to find a solution to this. Isn't that what they did with the Ebola outbreak, and that MRSA thing a little later? But the fire is different, and Jaxon thinks he knows why. It's happening too fast and too close. It's not a bunch of poor dark-skinned people in a faraway country getting burnt up first, so folks can't just sit back and donate money with their credit cards and put those little stamps of solidarity on the corners of their profile pics on social media. No, the fire is *here*, it's come directly for them and exploded right in their faces. So they're doing what they do best: lockdown. Instead of *Let's all work on this together*, the message is *We must protect our own.*

"In the wake of this terrible tragedy, we in Chicago would like to announce that we are suspending travel in and out of the city indefinitely," says the tinny voice over the radio. "Those who attempt illegal entry will be turned away, using force if necessary. Of course, we expect this to be only a temporary safety measure, and our thoughts and prayers are with the residents of those areas that have burned —"

"Yeah, thanks for the support," Artie grumbles, and flicks the radio off.

A rumble of agreement rolls through the small crowd gathered around the campfire. Jaxon had shied away the first time they laid the rocks down and lit match to dry tinder, but Lawrence laughed and patted him on the shoulder. *Don't you worry, son. We know what we're doing.*

He wasn't lying. When Artie and Jaxon finally made it up the mountain, covered in dust and soot, with barely half a bottle of water between them, they'd found the campground already occupied by the employees of Fire Station 19; they'd been in the middle of their annual family retreat when the city went up. Lawrence is their leader, a real-life fire captain, which is pretty cool.

Jaxon doesn't know the others very well yet, even though they've been here a while. Everyone's friendly, but whenever

Jaxon looks at them all he sees is his classmates burning up, or Mrs. Richardson, or the lady with her head on fire. Sometimes the thoughts get bad enough to make him sick again, so he tries to stay away from people in general.

The only person he's comfortable around is Artie. Jaxon doesn't have anyone else—Donte's in the ground, and they passed the blackened remains of the church on their way to the mountain, the church where Nana would've been in the middle of sorting old clothes and canned food, like she always did when Jaxon was at school. He left a note taped to the burnt wood of the church's front door just in case, but he's not so young as to hold out hope.

So here they are two weeks later, sleeping in tents while the city continues to burn down below. They talked about rescue the first few days, but that's dried up since the radio broadcasts made it clear: they're on their own. Which, to Jaxon, isn't actually new. Even before the fire and the worldwide swaths of death, he'd stopped believing in the government a long time ago. Nana probably said it best: *The world don't care about us, and we like it that way.* For the white folks in camp, it's probably a new thing, being abandoned. For people like Jaxon, it's really, really not.

Around the campfire, the conversation continues. "...igure it out," Lawrence is saying. "I mean, how does the fire pick who to burn?"

"Maybe it's not the people, it's the place," says one of the paramedics. "Did you hear the broadcast last night, about the fire that just died out in a hospital in Atlanta? It took a couple patients on one floor but that was it. The staff all came running for nothing."

"My cousin in Afghanistan says the same thing happened at his FOB," someone else adds. "Couple people went up at chow, everyone jumped on to put 'em out, and they all should've caught fire but none of 'em did."

"And then there's us," says a firefighter. "Those flaming cars came up the road the first few days, then nothing. No one here caught."

"Thank God for that."

"Maybe we were chosen for this, you know? The radio said there might be something special about—"

"Enough of that," Lawrence snaps. "Ain't no one here any more special or chosen or pretty-unique-snowflake than anybody else. You think like that and you might as well strike a match to yourself."

"Amen, brother."

Jaxon agrees. No one ever deserves to burn: not his classmates, not that lady on the street, not the millions already whose ash they breathe every day. That's why he didn't run away, two weeks ago when the fire started in the classroom. Nana didn't run when those angry men in white hoods tried to burn down the freedom bus she was riding on in '61. Donte didn't run when the bad guys were shooting at him in Iraq. It's just not in his blood, he supposes.

"You're thinking about him, aren't you?" Artie smiles down at him as the conversation around the campfire continues in the background, a soft, comforting buzz. "Your superhero."

He's not, but you never tell white folks they're wrong. Jaxon nods. "Yeah. Captain Fiero." He'd shown Artie the picture he drew when they first arrived in camp. He's not sure why, and he feels mostly embarrassed by it now. Captain Fiero seems so childish in the face of what they've seen.

"That's cool." Artie speaks around the granola bar he's eating; he always seems to have one sequestered somewhere on his person. "I've been meaning to ask you about how his powers work. Usually when you throw fire at fire, it just gets bigger. What makes Captain Fiero different?"

"Um." A strange mix of warmth and embarrassment gathers in Jaxon's stomach. He's pleased; no one's ever asked about Captain Fiero before, and all the other kids just laughed at his pictures and called him stupid. At the same time, what if he's wrong? About Captain Fiero's powers, about the good fire? What if Artie laughs at him too?

But Artie is just looking at him, chewing around an encouraging smile, and the man *did* save his life, so. "Well. Captain Fiero's fire isn't bad, not like the fire that burned everything up in town. His fire is good because it, um, it comes from his heart. It's made of his wanting to save people." It's sounding stupider and stupider by the moment. He ducks his head and mumbles the last few words. "So when his fire touches the bad fire, it puts it out."

"Oh." Jaxon's looking down at his feet so he doesn't see what kind of face Artie is making, but he doesn't sound like he's about to laugh or make sneering jokes. He just sounds curious. "So, back at your school...?"

"I had the good fire," Jaxon says, still not looking up. "I wanted to be like Captain Fiero, saving everyone, so I tried to put the other kids out because that's what he would've done. I think...I think maybe the bad fire sensed that, and that's why it skipped me. It didn't wanna mess with Captain Fiero."

"I see." It's hard to tell from his voice whether Artie actually does or not. He sounds distracted. Jaxon looks up and notices two things at once: one, Artie isn't watching him anymore, staring instead at the woods somewhere over Jaxon's shoulder.

Two, all movement in camp has stopped, everybody else staring in the same direction.

Very slowly, Jaxon turns.

The underbrush has birthed a man. Or at least, Jaxon thinks he's a man. It's hard to tell through all the smoke.

Because he's on fire.

Not *fire* fire, not like what happened in his classroom and then later through the entire city. But it's starting. The man stares at them with big, helpless eyes. Smoke pours from his clothes and his skin is a deep, angry red, like he spent too much time in the sun. He opens his mouth and croaks, "H-Help," and the word belches out around a fresh cloud of smoke.

Gasps all around. Several people back away as the man stumbles forward. Jaxon sees the fear in their eyes, the growing panic. A piece of the city, a clump of fiery infection suddenly invading their pristine haven. They should run. Bolt for the woods, hide away, save themselves. Let everyone else burn.

But that's not what Captain Fiero would do, is it?

"Help," the man begs again, just as something sparks and the top layer of his salt-and-pepper hair catches fire. Someone wails, and Jaxon can feel it in the air: the buzzing tension, the terror teetering on the brink of crumbling into chaos.

He doesn't even think about it, shooting to his feet and seizing his jacket. "Stop!"

He's not sure who he's talking to, but everyone obeys anyway. The man freezes, and all movement in camp halts. The couple of folks who had been edging toward the woods falter in their steps. All eyes go to him.

Jaxon lifts the jacket and steps toward the burning man. Tiny flames crown his hair and his breaths come high and panicked as he stares at Jaxon, but he doesn't move.

"*Son*," Lawrence hisses somewhere in the background, but Jaxon barely hears. He stops in front of the man, and they regard each other for a moment. The man's eyes are still full of panic, wide and near-crazy with it, and it would be so easy, Jaxon knows, to give in. He can feel it even now, the fear hovering on the edges of his consciousness. The bad fire is here, and it wants him to run.

But it didn't count on Captain Fiero, who has never said real words or breathed real air, but who lives in Jaxon nevertheless.

He looks up at the man, and it's surprisingly easy to smile. "I'm gonna put you out now," he says. Then he does just that: lifts up on his toes, throws his jacket over the man's smoking head, and pulls.

The man trips and falls to his knees with the momentum. Jaxon rolls with it, both of them tumbling to the dirt. Artie calls his name, but he ignores it as he quickly pats the jacket with his palms, just like he did back in the city two weeks ago. Except this time will be different. This time, he's not too late.

The man's body jerks beneath him, just like the lady's did before, and then goes still. The smell of something charred fills the air. Jaxon stares at the lump beneath his jacket, suddenly unsure. What if he's wrong? What if he lifts it up, and there's just more grey brains underneath?

Crunching footsteps, and Artie squats down next to him. His hand lands heavy on Jaxon's shoulder, but he doesn't say anything as he pinches a corner of the jacket and slowly lifts it up.

A few wisps of smoke and a pair of bright eyes greet them. The man coughs and shakes his head. Bits of burnt hair drift to the ground with the movement, and his scalp is all blotchy and pink and gross-looking, but he's alive.

He's alive.

Noise erupts all through camp. A million conversations get going at once, questions and exclamations and not a few prayers. Artie whistles. "Holy *shit*," he says, and before Jaxon can tell him that's a bad word, he gets a hearty clap to the shoulder. "Why didn't you run?" Artie asks.

And Jaxon can't really articulate it, not in the refined, sophisticated way it'll spread through the world over the next few days. He's only eight years old, after all, so he doesn't know fancy words like *valor* and *fortitude*. Right now, he only knows to look at Artie and say, "Because that's what the bad fire wants."

He sees it the moment Artie understands. His friend stands up and hurries over to the rest of the campers. Jaxon catches only bits and pieces of the conversation that follows, although one thing stands out above all: *spread the word.* People talk about putting a broadcast out on the radio, of putting an expedition together to head down to the city and tell everyone, tell the world. Start a new sort of sweeping conflagration.

They don't ask Jaxon to come, and he doesn't volunteer. He'll stay here a little while longer. He likes the quiet in these woods.

Something brushes his hand. Jaxon turns and it's the man he saved, reaching out with long, calloused fingers to wrap them around his own. The patches of skin that were burning before are now starting to blister, and he winces in pain with every movement, but when he squeezes Jaxon's hand, there is only softness in his eyes. "Thank you," he whispers.

Jaxon grins. He may not have a long red cape, or be able to make fireballs from his hands. He may not be tall, or handsome, or have lots of money or a big house or a pretty girlfriend, but right now, in his heart, he has the good fire.

See Kai Hudson's story "Combustion" online at Metaphorosis.
If you liked it, leave a comment. Authors love that!
Remember to subscribe to our e-mail updates so you'll know when new stories are posted.

About the story

Though it certainly doesn't read like one, "Combustion" is a pretty political piece for me. I kept seeing these terrible news stories about people mistreating other people (police shooting unarmed black men, countries turning away Syrian refugees, the violence of ISIS, etc.), yet political apathy and indifference seemed to be at an all-time high. My social media was full of posts and shares about these news stories, yet no one seemed to actually be *doing* anything. "Combustion" was born out of the frustration of being a witness to this phenomenon. If turning away from those who need help had the potential to actually kill us, would we be so quick to shut them out?

A question for the author

Q: Are titles easy or hard for you? Do you start with the title or the story?

A: Titles are pretty easy, mostly because I try to stay short and sweet. So long as it expresses the theme of my story, I'm good with it. I usually write the piece before I generate the title, but on at least one occasion I've written and planned an entire novel based on a title that came to me out of the blue one day. My muse works in mysterious ways.

About the author

Kai Hudson lives in sunny California where she writes, hikes, and spends entirely too much time daydreaming of far-off fantasy worlds.

Copyright

Metaphorosis Publishing

Metaphorosis offers beautifully written science fiction and fantasy. Our projects include:

Metaphorosis Magazine

Metaphorosis, a weekly magazine of SFF short stories, including stories from all the authors in this anthology. Find out more at magazine.metaphorosis.com, and sign up to be notified of new stories.

Metaphorosis Books

Recent books from Metaphorosis can be found at <u>books.metaphorosis.com</u>, and include:

Metaphorosis 2017

Metaphorosis 2016

All the stories from *Metaphorosis* magazine's second year.

Almost all the stories from *Metaphorosis* magazine's first year.

Metaphorosis: Best of 2017

The best science fiction and fantasy stories from *Metaphorosis'* 2nd year.

Metaphorosis: Best of 2016

The best science fiction and fantasy stories from *Metaphorosis'* 1st year.

Reading 5X5

Reading 5X5

Five stories, five times

Twenty-five SFF authors, five base stories, five versions of each – see how different writers take on the same material.

Writers' Edition

All the stories from the regular, readers' edition, plus two extra stories, the story seed, and authors' notes.

Best Vegan SFF of 2017

The best vegan science fiction and fantasy stories of 2017!

Best Vegan SFF of 2016

The best vegan science fiction and fantasy stories of 2016!

Susurrus

A darkly romantic story of magic, love, and suffering.

www.ingramcontent.com/pod-product-compliance
Lightning Source LLC
Chambersburg PA
CBHW020527120726
47904CB00003B/994